Little Black Girl Lost 4:
The Diary of Josephine Baptiste

Little Black Girl Lost 4:
The Diary of Josephine Baptiste

Keith Lee Johnson

www.urbanbooks.net

Urban Books
1199 Straight Path
West Babylon, NY 11704

Little Black Girl Lost 4: The Diary of Josephine Baptiste ©copyright 2009
Keith Lee Johnson

ISBN-13: 978-1-60162-149-8
ISBN-10: 1-60162-149-3

First Printing February 2009
Printed in the United States of America

10 9 8 7 6 5 4 3

Distributed by Kensington Publishing Corp.
Submit Wholesale Orders to:
Kensington Publishing Corp.
C/O Penguin Group (USA) Inc.
Attention: Order Processing
405 Murray Hill Parkway
East Rutherford, NJ 07073-2316
Phone: 1-800-526-0275
Fax: 1-800-227-9604

Dedication

To Lynn Osborne,
Thanks for writing, reading, and suggesting.
I wish all authors had fans like you.
You are a great one!

Acknowledgments

To Him, who is able to do considerably more than I can ask or think, I give you thanks.

To my wife: thanks for giving me the time to write, always knocking before entering my office, and cooking healthy meals when my health demanded it.

To my mom: thanks for teaching me to tell the truth from a very early age. It has been invaluable over the years. Thanks for all the motherly advice, the four o'clock in the morning conversations and the great food; especially the sweet potatoes.

Special thanks to my agent, Donald Maass. I didn't think we were going to get the deal done for *Little Black Girl Lost 4* and *5*. Due to your many years of experience, we were able to hammer a deal both parties could live with. Special thanks to your wonderful staff, particularly Cameron McClure and Stephan Barbara, who helped secure the audio rights to *PRETENSES*, *Sugar & Spice*, and *Fate's Redemption*.

Special thanks to Carl Weber for taking on all the *Little Black Girl Lost* novels.

To my man, Phillip Thomas Duck, author of *Playing with Destiny* and *Grown & Sexy*, in stores now: thanks for all the laughs you provide and the invaluable wisdom. I had a ball when you came to Toledo, bruh! But you forgot to remind me to write that story we talked about at BEA 2006 in Washington, DC. Shame on you!

To my good friend, Kendra Norman Bellamy, author of *Because of Grace* and *More than Grace*, in stores now: thanks for being a great woman of God and always having a godly, listening ear, and offering godly advice. It is always appreciated.

To Alisha Yvonne, author of *Lovin' You Is Wrong* and *I Don't Wanna Be Right*: thanks for being such a gracious and accommodating host when I was in Memphis. You definitely know how to get people to come to signings. Hopefully more authors will come to Memphis and see how the women in the South do things.

Special thanks to Tabitha, manager of Borders bookstore. Thanks for always looking out for me from the beginning. I won't forget you.

To all my coworkers who *bought* and read every single book: I can't thank you enough, and I appreciate each of you.

To all my fans: thanks for all the emails, and thanks so much for buying and reading *Little Black Girl Lost 1, 2,* and *3* and making them perennial Black Expressions bestsellers.

ACKNOWLEDGMENTS

To all the beauty salons in Toledo: thanks for allowing me to put stand-up posters in your shops.

And last but not least, special thanks to my man Fletcher Word of *The Sojourner's Truth* newspaper in Toledo, Ohio. BIG, BIG THANKS for all the articles and publicity.

"Pay more attention for free speech is high finance."
"Funkentelechy"
sung by
George Clinton of Parliament

During slavery there were several Negroes in the South, especially Louisiana and South Carolina, who would be accounted millionaires today. Most of them were slaveholders. These rich Negroes were treated in nearly every respect like white people. They could marry white wives—at least many of them did; they could buy white men and women—they did in Maryland and Louisiana until 1818, and in all probability, Florida, too; and even in the stage-coaches they did not ride Jim-Crow.

Joel Augustus Rogers
Sex and Race Volume II, p. 242 & 243. 1942.

Introduction

As many of you know from the last novel, the diary of Josephine Baptiste was finally delivered to me. I've read it several times. No matter how many times I read it, I'm always amazed, stunned even, at how one decision can change the course of a person's life and consequently, the course of an entire family unit. Such is the case with the Wise family. More than two hundred years ago, long before I, Johnnie Wise, was born, long before I met Lucas Matthews, Napoleon and Marla Bentley, George (Bubbles) Grant, the Beauregards (my white relatives), long before I talked Earl Shamus into purchasing a house for me in Ashland Estates, my great great grandmother rebelled against the wishes of her father and set her progeny on a collision course with a destiny that was riddled with hardship, disrespect, and ultimately murder.

My ancestors were never ever supposed to be a part of the Wise family; they were never ever supposed to be Americans; they most certainly were never to be of mixed blood. But because my great great grandmother, a free woman of Dahomey—modern day Benin, Nigeria—behaved foolishly in her native land, her imprudent splash in the ocean of life continues to ripple throughout time—today even.

If she had thought of someone other than herself; if she had thought about the consequences of her actions instead of dwelling on what she hoped would prove to be beneficial; if she had considered the benefits of the protective hedge of obedience before forging ahead into the abyss of uncertainty, I'm convinced that what happened to her, and what eventually happened to all the female family members born after her—those being Antoinette, Josephine, Marguerite, and me, Johnnie Wise—would never have happened to us.

Yet, I'm torn by her decision; torn by how it affected me and my own decisions. If the matriarch of our clan here in the Western Hemisphere doesn't rebel in the Eastern Hemisphere, am I born in New Orleans, Louisiana? Or am I born in Nigeria? Am I her first child? Or am I the last? More importantly, am I even alive to begin with? And if I am alive, am I who I am? If I am alive, am I of noble blood with all the privileges that accompany those who are? Or am I born at a time when my ancestors' land is pillaged and left destitute, leaving me in the same miserable condition as they found themselves? They say God works in mysterious ways. Given the way that my ancestors were brought to North America, I'd have to agree.

If she were alive today, I think Ibo Atikah Mustafa, my great great grandmother, would agree that the temptation to eat is sweeter than the eating itself. Unfortunately, she could not discern that truth from thinking of running away. Only the experience of running away could reveal the hidden nature of the temptation.

Thoughts of stealing away had first tickled her mind and then danced in her every imagination, making promises it could never deliver. Eventually, the temptation arrested and bound her hand and foot. Being in that state, fettered like a common criminal, much like Eve, the mother of all living, she too yielded. She *tasted*, and only then did she *see* her own folly; only then did she see how she was lured by her own ungoverned libido; only then did she understand that it was her own lust for the forbidden that landed her on the deck of a Dutch ship, a thousand miles from shore, making its way through the horrible corridors of The Middle Passage.

I can certainly sympathize with her and the rest of the women in my lineage.

For I, too, have behaved foolishly.

I, too, have rebelled and suffered the hardships of my own rebellion.

Hopefully, the diary of Josephine Baptiste, the fourth edition of the *Little Black Girl Lost* series, will shed some light on the plight of many women who, because of one selfish decision, suffer a lifetime of hardship.

Part 1

Hindsight

Chapter 1

Breaking the Spirit of a Man

She was more than startled, more than afraid when she heard a familiar but frightening sound. As she walked up the wooden stairs to the auction block, she was careful to never lock eyes with her pasty captors; a lesson that had been seared into her mind on the voyage to the Americas. She had seen the burgeoning crowd before coming out of her cell, and had heard the natives speaking in a language she clearly understood. They were bidding for the people who had been aboard the ship that brought them there. In her native land, she had seen people of her hue captured by those of the same and then sold, but without a bidding war. This was different.

She heard it again. This time she nearly jumped out of her skin. It sounded like the onslaught of ten thousand locusts buzzing as they neared a fertile and well-maintained, lush green garden. If only it were the sound of locusts coming to eat the season's crop. They would be far more welcome. The sound she heard was that of a well-crafted bullwhip as it neared a taut bare black back, before its tail broke the sound barrier and crackled loudly.

The sound forced an unpleasant memory to the surface. The first time she'd heard it was in Africa—Nigeria, to be exact. She could almost see the flesh-destroying weapon in her father's hand as he controlled captured enemies of Dahomey, her place of origin. The weapon didn't seem so frightening then. That was the way things were done, her father explained. Besides, the captured men were enemies who had tried to kill the men in their nation. The second time she heard the weapon was aboard the Windward, when the Dutch sailors used it on all the captives, even the women and children, to control them.

Now, in North America, more than four thousands miles from the shores of Africa, the sound alone made her tremble, though no one noticed. She stood perfectly still, attempting to hold on to a measure of pride in front of a crowd of pale onlookers. Of all the women who had been captured and sold, she was the only one who hadn't been raped or sodomized aboard the Windward.

Whoo! Whoo! Whoo!

She heard the horrifying sound again and lifted her eyes to look across the courtyard. Suddenly, the clamoring bidders standing a few feet from her were a distant memory as she zoned in on the barbarity. She saw a tall, well-built, tar black man having his flesh skillfully ripped away, exposing white flesh and bone, quickly followed by the flow of red blood. His wrists were stretched high above his head, tightly tied to a seven-foot pillar of white cement.

His torso was completely bare; his loins were covered by a pair of tight pants.

Whoo! Whoo! Whoo!

The sound of the whip hummed a familiar tune and then crackled again when it sliced into his back and peeled away more of his color, exposing more white meat underneath. About forty to fifty black men, women, and children who looked like him watched the chilling savagery with raw awe and indefinable dread. Next to them stood another fifteen or so white men and women, along with their children. Some of the women covered the children's eyes, turned their heads, and shook a little when each lash found an unmolested area of flesh. Others looked on nonchalantly, as if they had seen worse. But they hadn't. The truly horrifying part of it was yet to come.

Chapter 2

"Cause yo' mama and my mama be the same."

Still watching from the auction block, she saw a fashionably dressed black man who seemed to be in charge. He was wearing a navy blue suit, which consisted of breeches, a vest, a white silk shirt, a cravat, and white silk stockings. He stood near the black man wielding the whip.

Before delivering the next series of blows, the man with the whip wiped his face with a handkerchief. Sweat ran down his face as he doled out blow after blow, expertly turning the slave's back into a masterpiece of oozing red paint that made its way down his back.

A sound from deep within the slave climbed its way up his throat and out his mouth. It was the sound of agony mixed with humiliation. They had broken his will to resist, yet the fierce beating continued. With each stinging blow, he, being a grown man, was reduced to an infant, crying uncontrollably, unceasingly.

"Lord, God in heaven . . . Lord Jesus . . . help me!"

The man screamed, but the vicious beating continued. "No more, Massa Tresvant! No more! I'll be a good nigga, Massa! I swear to God, I'll be good."

Tresvant raised his hand, signaling the slave with the whip to stop the beating. "You're gonna stop reading my books?"

"Yes, Massa! I swear to the good Lord above I won't read another book for the rest of my life!"

"We'll just have to find out, won't we?" Tresvant said then nodded to the slave with the whip.

With the same intensity and ferocity—more, if it were possible—the whipping began anew. After several more lashes, the man's words became incoherent babble. With each stinging blow, he screamed and babbled until he could no longer stand. His knees surrendered and gave way, but his arms held him up.

Then mercifully, Tresvant said, "That's enough, Jude. Cut him down."

Jude took off his three-sided fedora and wiped his brow with his sleeve. He was of a small stature, taut, and light-skinned. He pulled a sharp knife from his boot, walked over to the demoralized slave and cut him down.

Tresvant looked at his other slaves and said, "You all know I hate doin' this, but he forced my hand. You all know that, right?"

Jude said, "Yes, Massa Tresvant. You sho' is right. You done gave that nigga plenty chances. He be too smart for his own good."

Tresvant said, "Don't I take good care of you all?"

In unison, they nodded quickly and repeated, saying, "Yes, Massa Tresvant."

Tresvant walked up to one of the white slave women

and said, "Dorothy, didn't I tell you this would happen when you asked me to buy him for you? I told you then he was smart and had runnin' in his eyes. I could see it even then. Didn't I tell you that?"

"Yes, Massa Tresvant," Dorothy said. "But Kimba is a good man. He just don't understand how things are here, Massa."

"Oh, he understands all right. All too well."

"Give him another chance, Massa. He gon' get his mind right. I'ma see to it."

"Why should I, Dorothy?" Tresvant said. "Give me one good reason why, and I might consider it."

"Cause yo' mama and my mama be the same. We's just got different poppas, is all. Yo' poppa be black and my poppa be white. Yo' poppa took my mama from my poppa 'cause he owned 'em. He had his way with her and she had you. Then he give her back to my poppa. Even though I be a slave, we still be blood; we still be sister and brother."

"You use that excuse every time, Dorothy," Tresvant said. "One day it's not gon' work. One day, I'ma hav'ta kill him." He turned to Jude. "Load 'em on the wagon and take him home." He looked at Dorothy. "Since you wanted me him to buy him for you, it'll be your responsibility to take care of his wounds. Get 'im back on his feet so he go back to work in the fields."

"Yessuh, Massa," Dorothy said.

The auctioneer spoke again, reminding the young woman on "stage" where she was and what was about to befall her. "This here is a fine specimen from the continent of Africa, gentlemen. And she already speaks English, French, Dutch, Spanish, and Portuguese. She can pick up other languages easily. It's a gift, I'm told. And gentlemen . . . she's still a virgin."

After the men heard that she hadn't been touched aboard the Windward, they murmured loudly, nodding their heads in approval, smiling lecherously.

"Let's start the bidding at eight hundred dollars," the auctioneer said.

One gentleman shouted, "Eight hundred dollars? For one slave? A wench, at that? Are you insane? I don't know that I'd pay that much for a prime studding buck, but I'd at least be more agreeable."

The auctioneer said, "Perhaps you didn't hear me, dear sir. Again, this one is different. She's practically royalty, sir. She was supposed to wed the son of a king where she's from. As I said, she already speaks English, Portuguese, Spanish, Dutch, and French, which means you won't have to spend months on end trying to get her to understand how things are. She already knows and can help the others understand much quicker. Not only would she make a good bed wench, but you can hire her out as an interpreter, sir."

"Eight twenty-five," a man in the crowd shouted.

"Eight fifty," said another

"Nine hundred," said yet another.

As the woman on the auction block looked into the faces of the men bidding for her, as she saw the lust in the eyes of her potential purchasers grow with each succeeding bid, she was sickened by it all. Suddenly, how it happened, how she ended up in a strange land, on sale to the highest bidder, rushed to her mind in powerful, vivid images.

Chapter 3

Young Love

Dahomey, Nigeria
The summer of 1791

It had happened to a chosen and pure gift from God that is great—that's what Ibo Atikah Mustafa means anyway. She was sixteen at the time. Her father had taken great care in naming her. Her name was not merely what she was called, but who she was supposed to be—a chosen and pure gift from God that is great! It happened to the seventh and last daughter of Jamilah, her father's first of three wives.

All the girls were gorgeous, but Ibo's beauty surpassed them all, and so did her intelligence. Her mind was a sponge. She quickly absorbed languages by listening to her father negotiate with the foreigners to whom he sold slaves. She was tall like her mother, about six feet, athletic, and thick all over—the picture of health and perfection. Her skin was flawless, the color of russet. She was an untouched, unblemished maiden, engaged to the eldest son of the king—heir to the throne.

It happened the night before the wedding celebration. Ibo was so impressionable and so young when it happened. She was a child. And like many children, she was incredibly spoiled, used to having her way at all times. She pouted whenever Faisal, her father, who was strict, overruled her permissive mother.

Faisal blamed Jamilah for giving Ibo so much freedom. She was supposed to train her to be a certain kind of woman, a certain kind of wife. Jamilah's training was successful for the most part, but Ibo was also a rebel, just as her father had been in his youth. The greatest of her flaws was conceit.

Although Ibo wore a veil in the city when she went out with her older sisters, she could bewitch a man with a single glance. Because of the veil, all they could see were her brown eyes, which were soft yet penetrating, and extremely alluring. Men stopped whatever they were doing, stared mindlessly, and dreamed of bedding her. Even women stared robotically. When she locked eyes with people, it was as if they were compelled to look at her, until she looked away, releasing them from momentary captivity. She knew early on that she had a special power over people; everyone except her ambitious father—and Amir Bashir Jibril.

The spell that Ibo cast on men and women alike was identical to what she experienced when she looked at Amir. He was tall and wonderfully built, with hard, solid muscles; beautiful to behold. His hair was full of soft curls that rode his broad shoulders. He cast a spell on her, she knew. And she loved it. From the moment she saw him, she was overcome with emotions she couldn't begin to understand. She only knew that whenever she looked at him, she was enraptured by a wave of emotions.

The feeling of euphoria stayed with her long after he was no longer near. She often wished he was a cool drink of water, so that she could drink all of him. One glimpse of him was enough to make her daydream for hours about what it would be like to marry him instead of Adesola, his brother, who was the same age as her father.

In his youth, Faisal had been a farmer like his father. He wanted more, and struck out on his own after he saw his father sell one of his debtors to the Portuguese traders for alcohol and tobacco. Unlike the Prodigal Son from the Bible, Faisal left home with nothing and became a slaver when he was twenty years old. Now, at fifty-one, he was one of the richest men in Dahomey. His three wives and forty-one children lived on his father's sprawling farm, which he expanded to ten times its original size.

Faisal had everything a wealthy man could afford, yet he still wanted more. He wanted to be the king, but he hadn't been born into the royal family. He could, however, acquire a seat on the king's court for a price: his youngest daughter from Jamilah, Ibo Atikah Mustafa. To him, she was a small price, and he was all too willing to pay. It would be good for her, he reasoned selfishly, because she could serve as the king's interpreter, making him privy to private conversations of a personal and political nature. Unfortunately for Faisal, Ibo and Amir had another plan.

Chapter 4

A Daring Escape

It was midnight and the festivities celebrating Ibo's last night as a maiden had ended nearly two hours earlier. Tradition required that her mother and sisters spend the entire night together—a bachelorette's party of sorts. Timing was everything. It was difficult to be patient, but she knew she had to be. She would only have one chance. If she made her move too soon, she would be caught, and all her plans would be thwarted by one of her sisters, or perhaps her mother, before she made the first step that would free her of the familial obligation.

Marrying Adesola was never a consideration. Going along with her father's plans was the cover she and Amir used while they planned to run away together to Sierra Leone, where he would learn to build ships.

She would wait until they all entered the dream world before making her escape.

The night dragged on and on, seeming to go on forever. It seemed as if the women would chat all night. Nevertheless, she put on a good show for them, smiling, laughing even. They all believed that she was happy, that she was looking forward to the ceremony.

It wasn't all a show, though. The smiles bubbled to the surface because she had thought of Amir and running away all night. The laughing came from knowing she had outwitted them all, including her mother, who was usually more discerning.

Hearing light snoring throughout the room, she opened her eyes, squinted, attempting to see her mother, who was only a few feet away, sleeping on a rug Ibo made and gave to her as a birthday present a couple of years earlier.

Jamilah was asleep, she could see. She knew that this was her opportunity to flee and meet Amir. It was now or never. Her heart pounded so hard she thought it would burst. She remained perfectly still as she allowed her eyes to adjust to the darkness. She would never forgive herself if, in her haste, she tripped over someone, woke them, and missed the chance that would never come again.

She saw her sisters and aunts scattered throughout the room, making it difficult to find an easy path to the covered door opening. She looked at the open window, which was closer, but much more intimidating, since her mother was sleeping beneath it.

As quietly as she could, she stood up then waited a few seconds, just in case someone heard her. If it were possible, her heart pounded harder, louder, like someone was beating a bass drum. She stole a quick breath, attempting to calm her frayed nerves. She looked down at Jamilah again, afraid her mother would suddenly wake up. She wanted to take the first step, but it was the hardest.

Standing there, looking at her mother for what might very well be the last time, she thought seriously about changing her mind and going through with the wedding. But when she thought of Amir, she knew she couldn't disappoint him. She knew he was waiting. He was taking the greatest chance of all because if they were caught, the king would have him beheaded. He had put his life on the line for her, and she had to be at least willing to meet him at the edge of their property as agreed.

She lifted her foot several times before returning it to its original spot. Each time she lifted it, it shook uncontrollably. Again she considered lying back down and forgetting about her plans of escape. A lesser woman would have. Again she knew she couldn't disappoint Amir. Again she found the strength to leave all that she had ever known.

Time was running out. It would be dawn in a couple hours. Amir had told her they needed at least a two-hour head start or they would be caught. She lifted her foot again and it shook again, but this time, she made the all-important first step. She was so scared that her knees almost gave way and let her fall on her backside.

By sheer will, she steadied herself and made another step. It was easier than the first. She was standing right next to her mother now—her heart pounding feverishly, on the verge of exploding. All she had to do was step over her mother and she would be free.

She stole another quick breath and held it. Quietly, she stepped over her mother, leaving one foot behind.

She looked down at her mother, saying within, "Please, Mama, don't wake up."

Jamilah didn't move. She didn't know her youngest daughter was making a clandestine departure. She didn't know that her memories would be all she would ever have, and slept the moment away.

Ibo pulled the foot she had left behind over her mother, still looking down at her, still hoping she wouldn't wake up and catch her. She waited a few more precious seconds and then hoisted herself up on the open window. She looked for the last time at her mother, and then made her escape.

Chapter 5

"Trust him, my son."

Amir Bashir Jibril was half Nigerian and half Egyptian. He was born of a highly educated Egyptian woman named Asenath, which means *she belongs to her father*. Amir Bashir Jibril means *prince, bringer of good news*, and *archangel*, in that order. He was to be all that his name embodied.

Amir was indeed a prince, but he was only one of many, being the seventh son of the fifth wife. But as far as ruling the kingdom was concerned, he was far from the throne in the line of succession; nor did he want to rule it. He had but two ambitions. The first was to be a master shipbuilder. The second was to marry a woman he truly loved.

He had seen how the king, his father, treated his mother, only calling for her when he needed fulfillment; then, having sown his royal seed, sent her back to her house to wait for the urge to hit him again. The fifth wife had another burden to bear; she was not only ruled by the desires of the king, but wives one through four had authority over her too. While she had her own house, her own servants, she almost never saw her husband, the king, and consequently, Amir rarely saw his father. He thought that if being a king made it easy to neglect one of his wives, it wasn't something he aspired to be. He was glad that he, in all likelihood, would never be in a position to ignore the family he had sired.

Knowing his journey with Ibo would be one in which sleep would be a luxury he could ill afford much of, he had gone to bed early. At only eighteen, he was chosen to be one of the king's most prized warriors. Though he possessed the body of a god, he knew the value of rest before a battle. Rest, along with the proper shoes and weapons, always made the difference on the field of battle.

The ingredient that made him a resolute warrior was not the great strength he possessed, but his God-given speed, his indomitable spirit, and his unyielding mind. Speed of foot, speed of hand, and great coordination were but a few of his allies, and they served him well in the heat of battle. Armed with sword and shield, he could easily defeat ten men. Having proven himself to his older contemporaries, he was quickly promoted to captain of the infantry.

"Wake up, my son," his mother called out to him from across the room. Amir was Asenath's favorite son of the seven she bore. "The moon is full and you must be on your way soon."

Amir opened his eyes, but didn't respond.

"Arise and eat, my son," Asenath called out. "You will need to have all your strength."

Amir gathered himself, stood up, and walked over to the basin and washed his face and hands. Afterward, he went over to the table she prepared for him and sat down. He reached for some of the ripe, sweet-smelling fruit she had cut up. He was about to put a cube of pineapple in his mouth when he heard his mother's silent voice telling him to stop with only the feeling of a daunting stare.

"Let us thank the Lord God of Israel for his goodness," she said.

When she finished her humble supplication, with noticeable cynicism, Amir, unconvinced of spiritual things, said, "Will your Lord God of Israel be with me and my bride on our journey, my mother?"

"I have prayed for this very thing, my son."

Amir studied her as she spoke, wondering if she herself believed the unbelievable things she often spoke of. "So we shall be safe? Nothing evil will befall us?"

Asenath exhaled softly and gathered her patience. "The Lord God doesn't guarantee you a life without trouble. He only promises to be with you and never leave you through whatever trouble comes your way. Trust him, my son."

Chapter 6

"So you're ready to die then, my mother?"

Amir rolled his eyes and said, "Hmpf, my spear, my sword, and my shield . . . these are the things I trust. These are the things that I can see and feel. As for your Lord God of Israel, have you at any time seen or at least touched him? Ever?"

Angry now, Asenath frowned and asked, "Have you at any time seen or at least touched your brain? Ever?"

Amir looked away.

"The Lord God of Israel will be with you through all your hardships as he has been with me through mine," Asenath said with confidence.

Amir frowned. "Wouldn't it be better if your God never let the trouble come your way in the first place?"

"My son, hear me and understand . . . all sunshine makes a desert."

"But mother, the king will kill you when he realizes

that I have gone with Ibo to your brother's land, will he not?"

Asenath shrugged her shoulders and said, "I suppose he will, my son."

Frustrated and angry about her nonchalant attitude concerning her own death, he blurted out, "Are you not afraid?"

She walked over to her son and kissed the back of his head. "Oh, Amir, it so sweet of you to worry about me." She returned to her seat. "And yes, when the king realizes that I have plotted against him, he will seek my life. But what he doesn't know is that he'll be setting me free from this bondage that I have endured for more than thirty years."

With resignation, he said, "So you're ready to die then, my mother? You're ready to give your life so that I can have a chance at mine?"

At eighteen, Amir was far too young to know the things he thought he knew. He didn't know nor did he understand that his mother had been in captivity for thirty long years. He didn't know nor did he understand that she was far too tired to care about the king and what he might do because of her betrayal. She was sick and tired of being a kept woman, living a life without the passion that romantic love delivers. Death had no hold, no power over her because she had died a long time ago.

Amir had been her only reason for living. Now that he had found a woman worthy to take her place, death was a welcomed guest in her house of life. To be killed so that her favorite son could have a woman he was willing to die for was an honor that warranted reciprocation. He was too young to understand that she would never throw her life away frivolously. Her decision to expire was made with much contemplation and reflection. She wasn't casting her life aside on a whimsical flight of fancy; she was offering it on the altar of sacrifice as a final act of love.

With stone-faced conviction, she said, "I am."

The thought of his mother's death troubled his soul, and had become unbearable. As the time of his furtive departure approached, he thought he could persuade her to leave with them. But his pleas were met by an impenetrable wall of resistance. Now that the hour of his exodus had arrived, leaving her in the hands of her unforgiving husband was more difficult than he imagined.

"But how can I live, how can I be happy with my bride knowing my happiness cost you your life?"

"You know that I am a daughter of Egypt; a daughter of wealth and influence?"

Exasperated, he said, "Yes, mother. You have told me this many times."

"But I never told you how I came to this land, did I?"

"No, my mother, you did not. Please tell me now. Help me understand your willingness to die without a fight."

Asenath knew that her death would torture him for some time to come. She opened her arms and beckoned him to her bosom. He went to her and kneeled. She took his head with both her hands and pulled it to her chest. With her arms, she embraced his head and held on, for she, too, was tormented by their separation.

"Amir . . . please understand that love . . . true love . . .

is boundless." She sighed. "When a woman falls in love, she'll do anything for the man she loves. It is like being under the spell of a powerful sorcerer. When I fell in love with Boaz, who was the son of a close friend and business acquaintance of my father's, he forbade me to see him. Boaz, like his father, was an unorthodox Jew, trusting in Christ for the redeeming of their eternal souls. They looked like many of our Egyptian brothers and sisters, having rich mahogany skin like you.

"I loved my father, and up to that time, I had never defied him. But Boaz was so handsome, so incredibly kind, that I could not bear the thought of never seeing him, never being his wife, never having his children.

"Boaz's father felt the same way. Islam and Christianity couldn't co-exist. They could do business together, but I soon learned that was where it ended. The very idea of Boaz and I being in love ruined my father's relationship with Boaz's father.

"Like you and Ibo, we had planned to run away together. I wanted to meet Boaz. I did. I truly loved him, but when the time came to meet him, my courage abandoned me."

Amir raised his head from her chest and looked into her eyes. "I don't understand, my mother. If you loved him, why didn't you go to him? Why did you let fear consume you?"

She pulled his head to her chest again. "I thought about the life my father provided. We had a beautiful home, servants, and wanted for nothing. With Boaz, life would have been uncertain. We would have been on the run. Family was everything. It was all I knew. I was comfortable. Secure. Going with Boaz would have changed everything. When I considered these things, I lost heart.

"Instead of meeting him the night that we were to take flight, I stayed in bed. I prayed all night that the Lord God of Israel would let him know why I couldn't run away with him.

"A few days later, I was whisked away in the middle of the night on a caravan to this place. My father, whom I loved dearly, told me I was to be the wife of a king who believed in Islam as he did.

"What my father didn't know was that I had already converted and was committed to Judaism. He didn't know that I had been given a copy of an original King James Version Bible, first published in 1611.

"Now, some thirty years later, Ibo is forced to make the same choices that were set before me. I hope for your sake that she possesses the courage I did not have. That night clings to me like the heaviness of a block of steel. For more than thirty years I have relived that night, wishing I could change my mind, knowing I never could. And so . . . when the king takes my life—and I pray to the Lord God he will—I will finally be free. I will die with the knowledge that my favorite son had the chance to be with the woman he loved."

Finally, understanding was threatening to breach his dull psyche and teach him the things a woman hides deep in her heart. He raised his head again and searched his mother's eyes as fear crept into his mind. "Do you think Ibo is thinking of not meeting me?"

"I'm sure of it. Even as we speak, she is struggling with

the idea of leaving mother and father, sisters and brothers, all that she has ever known. And for what? A future that does not yet exist? She is to be married to the prince tomorrow who will soon be king. What can you offer her other than a dream?

"So you see, my son, she has to have a great love for you to leave security and peace of mind. She loves a man who may be hunted down and killed in her presence. This is the position you have put her in. I have prayed that the Lord God grants you peace and riches, but know that they will come at a price."

He lowered his eyes and reflectively said, "If she meets me, I will give her the chance to change her mind."

"See that you do, my son. She will love you all the more for doing so."

Chapter 7

"Will we be happy? Please tell me we will."

It was unseasonably cool the night that Ibo Atikah Mustafa made her way down the dirt road leading to the man she loved with all her heart. She was almost there, almost at the end of the property, where Amir would meet her. Fear and exhilaration grew when she heard his prized black Arabian snort. Moving faster now, with a sense of urgency, she walked toward the images she saw in the moonlight.

It was Amir. He, too, had made his escape. She could see him now, arrayed in battle gear which consisted of a leather vest and kilt; his sword was in its sheath around his waist. His shield and spear was resting harmlessly on his horse. Closer now, she could see that there were two horses, not just one. Overwhelmed by an avalanche of emotions, she ran to him and fell into his open arms.

"Come, now, my love," Amir began, whispering, cognizant that they were in mortal danger as long as they were in their country of origin. "We dare not linger here. We have but an hour or two at most before they discover your absence."

"Oh, Amir, Amir," Ibo uttered breathlessly. "Can't you just hold me . . . if only for an instant? I have looked forward to this moment for so very long."

"Only for a second longer, my love. Our lives are but grass to the king. And he will not spare us. Let us be as the wind . . . strong, silent, and free to roam wherever it wills. Let us be gone."

She sighed. "To the sea?"

"Yes, to the sea, where I will build my own fortune."

"And where we will marry and have children?"

"Many children, my love." He got on the Arabian and extended his hand to help her onto the horse. "Come, we dare not tempt fate a second longer. Food, water, clothing, everything we need, I have brought with me."

"Do you think your mother will tell where we went?" Ibo asked.

"Eventually. She will hold out for as long as she can before telling the king." The thought of his mother being tortured mercilessly filled his heart and his countenance fell.

He changed the subject. "She has made you a lovely wedding garment and lots of other silks and fine linens you'll love. Besides, she thinks we're going south, to Lagos, where her brother lives. We're going west, where I will show you the ocean of life."

Her arms were wrapped around his waist. She

squeezed, wishing she could somehow become a part of him at that moment. "Did you remember to thank her for me?"

"I did remember," Amir replied. There was a hint of sadness in his voice.

"It was hard leaving her, huh?"

"Harder than it was for you to leave your mother, my love. My mother will die tomorrow—or worse, be tortured for days and then murdered. All because she knew of our plot to leave this land and dwell in one of our own. I hated deceiving her."

She loosened her grip and looked at the back of his head. "How did you deceive her?"

"My love, I have told you this already. I told her we were going to live with her brother in Lagos. I told her this knowing the king will force her to tell everything she knows. Because she believed me, the king will believe her and go three days' journey in the wrong direction. This, my love, will secure our escape and more important, our happiness.

"If I'm right, if they believe my mother, they will never find us, and we can never ever return to this place. So decide now. Are you ready for this? Or do you want to remain here and be the wife of a king?"

Without hesitation, Ibo said, "I'm ready for this. I will be the wife of a prince." She wrapped her arms around his waist and laid her head on his back. "Oh, Amir. I love you so. Will we be happy? Please tell me we will."

"We will never be happier than we are at this moment, my love. Remember it, for you will tell of it to our daughters and our sons. They will know that we risked all for the sake of love. Because of what we do tonight, our children will know that it is wrong to have a mate chosen for them. They will have a mate of their own choosing."

With his bride safely behind him, he gently kicked the sides of his Arabian and led him over to the other horse. He reached out and grabbed the rope that was tied to the reins and they galloped away. Amir had made Ibo feel so safe and secure that as they rode off together in the moonlit night, she told herself that she would love him forever.

In five days they would be safe on the seashores of Sierra Leone—at least that's what they thought.

Chapter 8

They had no plan of escape.

The dawn of a new day was approaching as the darkness gave way to illumination. They had driven the horses hard and only rested them for a short while when they could. After three long days and nights of running from their land of origin, they took refuge near a bank of fresh water. They filled their cisterns, ate the delicious fruit and nuts Amir's mother had packed. Ibo used their oasis as a chance to see the clothing Asenath made for her. Asenath was a very stylish and classy woman.

The silks and linens fit her like a glove. The garments helped her forget about what had happened to her soon-to-be mother-in-law.

After she tried on all the garments and paraded around so Amir could appreciate her in them, they talked of fulfilling their dreams in Sierra Leone until they fell asleep in each other's arms.

While they were sleeping near a pond, Ibo was awakened by what smelled like Dutchmen—slavers. She knew their scent, as she had smelled it many times. She sniffed a few more times, and when she was certain, she opened her eyes to warn Amir, who hadn't slept since they left three days earlier.

She shook Amir and he opened his eyes, but sleep was still upon him. She put her index finger to her lips, warning him not to make a sound. In the distance she heard the Dutchmen speaking in their native tongue.

She listened to them. They were much closer than she originally thought. They were coming to fill up their cisterns and then they would be on their way to their ship with a haul of procured slaves.

"How much do ya think we'll get for this quiver of niggers, Cap'em?" a man said.

"It depends on how many of them survive the voyage."

Ibo's eyes bulged when she heard the man who responded to the question. Her belly did flip-flops. She knew him. Her father did business with him, and he had tried many times to buy her.

When Amir saw how scared she was, he raised his head up and said, "What's wrong, my love?"

Ibo quickly stood to her feet and gathered their belongings. "Amir, we must go! They're coming!"

His mind was still in a fog when he said, "Who's coming? What are you so afraid of? We are two days' journey from our new home. We're free, my love."

"No, Amir! It's Captain Rutgers! He wants me!"

"He wants you? What do you mean, he wants you?"

"I can explain everything to you later, but now, we must go!"

Amir didn't understand the urgency and for that reason, he moved like he had all the time in the world, like there was no immediate danger. Being up for three days and three nights is no easy task. It requires the strictest discipline; if not that, the hot pursuit of men who want nothing more than to take his head off at the shoulders.

Seventy-two hours of vigilance had worn him out. He wanted to sleep for at least another hour or two. He was sure he had earned it. He looked at Ibo. She was already on the Arabian, ready to take flight again.

"Well, well, well," Captain Rutgers said after recognizing Ibo. He had found her incredibly attractive and intelligent. As much as he wanted to enter her folds and take as much pleasure as her unwilling body gave, he knew she would be worth so much more if her hymen was intact once they reached the shores of the Americas. An intact hymen and her extraordinary gift of languages could easily fetch a tidy sum; perhaps five or six thousand at the auction block in New Orleans.

When Amir heard the man's voice, instinctively he turned toward it and saw about twenty or so white men with flintlock pistols and rifles. With them, he saw about a hundred or more naked black men, women, and children. Most of the men were in wooden yolks. The women and child wore collars of iron. They were all chained together. He looked into their eyes and saw defeat. They had given up, given in to their captors. They had no plan of escape.

Chapter 9

"Don't hurt the girl."

Amir looked at his Arabian, where Ibo sat, and where his spear and shield hung. They were about thirty feet away. He had depended on his speed to gain the advantage in battle before. It had served him well. Now, however, the speed of a steel ball trumped being fleet of foot. But still, his warrior's spirit wondered what his chances were of getting to his weapons before they fired theirs.

As he thought of running to his horse and retrieving the weapons, still calculating his odds for success, it occurred to him that they wouldn't shoot. They were slavers. He and his precious Ibo were the prizes.

Ibo looked at Amir. She could tell by the way he kept looking at his weapons and the Dutchmen that he was going make a stand; he was going to fight for her, for them, for their God-given right to freedom. She knew he would die if necessary, which gave her confidence. They would both fight and die before becoming the property of mere mortals.

Without further delay, believing that the Dutchmen wanting to enslave him increased his chances of surviving because no bullets would be fired, he ran to his Arabian. In the blink of an eye, he had his shield and spear, ready for action, ready to kill or be killed.

"Don't hurt the girl," Captain Rutgers yelled out. "Try not to damage the prince. They're both worth a small fortune."

When Ibo heard that, she became even more confident, knowing they had been given strict orders not to harm her. She grabbed Amir's princely sword and slid it out of the sheath.

When the captured Africans saw Amir and Ibo taking a stance, they found the strength to resist too. They started chanting like warriors, shaking their chains—the women and children too.

Captain Rutgers gave orders for half his men to control the slaves and half to capture the man and woman. "No matter what, don't harm the girl in any way!" he yelled.

Amir and Ibo ran at the Dutchmen, catching them off guard.

Ibo screamed in Dutch, "Dood aan de witte man!"

Amir screamed the same thing, having no idea that he was saying, "Death to the white man!"

The Dutch slavers were so surprised by their sudden offensive that they stood still and watched the man and woman run at full speed, screaming, "Dood aan de witte man!" They didn't start fighting back until one of their shipmates had been run through with Amir's spear. He died instantly.

Being fleet of foot, Amir quickly killed five Dutch slavers in a matter of seconds, using his shield and his spear. He slashed through throats, broke noses with his shield so quickly that the slavers didn't have a chance to respond to his rapid movements. After running through yet another slaver with his spear, he pulled it out of his victim and threw it. It sailed fifty feet in the air before striking its target—one of the slavers who were trying to control the men and women in chains. The head of the spear pierced the back of his neck and came out the front.

The captured slaves fought with the Dutchmen as best they could.

Ibo, with one clean slash, cut the carotid artery of a slaver. But when she saw his blood pumping out of his body, she suddenly became a statue, frozen solid by what she saw.

The slaver put his hand to his throat, pulled it away, and looked at his own blood. His eyes looked as if they no longer contained life. The blood was still pumping out of his neck, running down the front of his shirt, splashing down on the ground, making a small pond. He dropped to his knees. Once there, he fell face first onto the ground, dead.

One of the slavers was so enraged by seeing the death of his best friend that he ignored his orders and pointed his flintlock rifle at Ibo's head. What was the death of one nigger wench? It was about revenge for his friend, and he would have it in one second's time. He was just about to pull the trigger when he heard a small explosion. Time stopped for a split second as he realized that he was shot in the head by Captain Rutgers. A split second later, he fell forward, dead.

When Ibo heard the shot, she whipped her head around to see what had happened. The slaver who was about to shoot her had been shot in the eye by Captain Rutgers. It was the second time she'd ever seen someone get killed. Seeing two dead men took all the fight she had out of her. She stood still, frozen, looking at him, unable to believe what she had seen.

Suddenly, she heard footsteps—running footsteps. They were almost upon her. By the time she turned to see what was happening, she was tackled by Captain Rutgers. She hit her head on the ground. Everything went black.

Chapter 10

"Where's the prince? Is he alive?"

Before she was fully conscious, she heard the creaking of the ship, the roar of the waves, gusts of wind. She felt the movement of the vessel, but had no idea she was aboard the Windward. The heat of the sun blazed through one of the windows, letting her know it was daylight. Suddenly, pain impulses registered and increased at the back of her skull, throbbing with each beat of her heart. She frowned and tried to swallow. Her throat was dry and needed fresh water to make it possible to talk above the level of whispering.

She opened her eyes and took in the luxury the cabin offered. She found the white curtains covering the window particularly attractive as she scanned the room. The enormous number of books that lined the walls stood out far more than anything else.

"I thought I had lost you," Captain Rutgers said. He

was having lunch, which consisted of roasted chicken, rice, green beans, bread, and white wine.

She whipped her head in the direction of the voice and saw him. In Dutch, she whispered, "Water."

Rutgers went over to his private dining table, where a glass pitcher full of clear water sat. He picked up a glass and poured the water in and then went over to the bed and sat down. He then helped Ibo rise up to drink.

"Slowly now," he said. "You've been in and out of consciousness for four days now." When she began to guzzle, Rutgers pulled the glass away from her and laid her back down. "You can have more later."

In a raspy voice, she said, "Amir. Prince Amir. Where is he?"

Rutgers smiled. "Ah . . . young love. There's nothing like it."

Ibo frowned and summoned all the strength she had, which was very little, and raised herself up from the bed. "Where is he, Captain Rutgers?"

"So you remember me. Good. Good. We will have lots of time to talk. We have a long voyage ahead of us. We will get to know each other well."

When she saw the lust in his eyes, she pulled the covers up to her neck, which was when she realized she was completely nude under the sheet.

She locked eyes with him. "No, you must not. I am a maiden. The prince's maiden. He will take your head."

"Where you're going, titles won't mean anything. Might as well get used to it now. You're my property, and I can do with you as I like. It just so happens that I did not violate you in any way. Your price will be of greater value at the auction on the Isle of Santo Domingo."

She stared at him for a moment or two, amazed he hadn't taken her. She had seen his wanton gaze many times. "I am to be sold?"

With a sinister sneer, Rutgers said, "Disappointed that it won't be me who deflowers you, eh?" He laughed uproariously. "It won't be Prince Amir either. Get it outta your head. The adjustment will go smoother if you do."

"Where's the prince?" she asked desperately, wondering what became of him. "Is he alive?"

Chapter 11

A Breathtaking View

The smile Rutgers wore vanished in an instant when he thought of all the men the prince had killed prior to being captured. He could still see the prince breaking necks, snatching out throats with speed and power, long before his men knew what was happening to them.

"Slightly damaged. But yes, very much so. He, too, will fetch a great price."

"I want to see him," she said, staring unrelentingly into his eyes.

"All in good time, dear girl," Rutgers said and continued eating. He swallowed his food and drank from his wineglass. Then he wiped his mouth with a white tablecloth. With extreme politeness and respect, he said, "Before we do, let's get you dressed and fed and then we shall see your prince, okay?"

Ibo answered with a slight but begrudging nod, letting

him know she would cooperate, but with uncompromising restraint and with tightly tied strings attached.

Rutgers picked up a silver dinner bell and shook it. A few seconds later someone knocked on the door.

"Come," Rutgers said in a commanding tone.

A shipman opened the door and said, "Yes, Captain?"

Still devouring his food, Rutgers said, "Bring our guest something to eat and bring the special cargo I've selected up on deck for a bit of exercise."

"Shall I include the prince, sir?"

"Especially the prince," Rutgers said without looking at the shipman. "Make sure you clean him up and give him his clothes."

The shipman nodded and said, "Very good, sir." He closed the door.

Rutgers waited until he heard footsteps going away from the cabin before looking at his young captive. "You'll find your clothes in that chest underneath the portside window." He showed her with his eyes. "When you've finished eating, we'll have a talk with the prince."

He stood up to leave, then turned around and said, "There is no escaping me or this vessel. We are at sea, and you couldn't possibly swim to shore even if you knew how; even if you were the best swimmer that ever lived." He smiled and continued, "Besides, the water is full of man-eating sharks, and they would love to eat a beautiful creature like you if you happened to fall in the water.

"If you need anything, ring the bell as you've seen me do, and the guard will get it for you. Do not attempt to leave this cabin for any reason without checking with the guard. He will find me, and I'll give him instructions concerning you. Do you understand?"

She answered him with a quick nod.

Ibo had no idea what a shark was, but she did understand that if she jumped into the water, she would be eaten alive by something. What Captain Rutgers didn't know was that if he had told her the prince was dead, she would not have cared to live another moment without him and would have flung herself overboard at the first opportunity. Since the prince was alive, she, too, would stay alive.

Later, when she had time to think, she would work out a plan of escape. Though she and Amir were to be someone's property in a strange land with strange customs, she didn't allow those thoughts to subdue her optimism. Seeing the prince was all she could think of. Amir would think of something, she was sure.

An hour later, Ibo and the man who guarded her climbed the stairs and stepped onto the deck. The heat was blazing; the sun unrelenting, singeing her skin, causing her to squint her eyes in defense. She was expecting to see Amir, but instead, she saw something that took her breath away.

Chapter 12

"You're about to enter a world where your life has little to no value."

Ibo stepped onto the deck dressed in pure Egyptian purple silk; the kind that was fit only for an upper class woman from that culturally rich land. She was absolutely magnificent to look upon, and her mannerisms, although subtle, offered an aura of nobility. Her deep set eyes captured them all and stopped all movement—even time itself, it seemed, as she stood perfectly still, taking in the effect she had on everyone who could see her. A cacophony of quiet arose and remained. It was as if God himself said, "Quiet yourselves and behold my glory as I pass by." Only the roar of the sea could be heard at that moment.

At least a hundred men, women, and children seemed to be waiting for her arrival; as if her arrival would be that of a majestic empress whose presence demanded that her subjects wait patiently, and not that of a common slave. All of them were completely nude, and embarrassed, it appeared, as each of them lowered their heads and covered their exposed genitals when she looked at them. The children, some of them teens, others much younger, attempted to hide their privates too. They were all wearing chains around their necks, hands, and ankles. When they moved, the clanging of the chains rang out loudly.

A southerly wind blew their scent into her nose. She suddenly felt an immediate need to throw up all that she had eaten. Violently, what she had ingested rushed its way out of her stomach, through her esophagus, and out her mouth, landing on the deck and on the perfectly fitted purple silk garment Amir's mother had made. The smell of her vomit was so vile that she fell to her knees and threw up again. Mocking laughter from the Windward crew filled her ears and rang in her mind.

She heard chains clanging together. When she looked up, she saw the nude men and women parting, making room for another. She watched as the sea of people parted until she saw him—Amir.

He stood tall, brave, and proud; his spirit and will intact, defiant, unlike the other captives who were far more subdued. He was wearing his princely uniform. The strong wind caused his black cape to flap against his fettered bronze ankles. His feet were shoulder width apart, providing perfect balance, presenting a strong and powerful mystique, even though he, too, was a captive. He gazed into Ibo's soft eyes, penetrating them, telling her without saying a single word to remember who she was, where she came from, who she belonged to.

In an instant, Ibo remembered all that Amir's eyes said. She gathered herself and stood up, determined to be equally defiant, equally proud, equally unshakable.

"Beslis," Ibo heard Captain Rutgers call out. *Decide*, she understood immediately, translating the word without thought. *Decide what?* she wondered.

She looked at Rutgers; her eyes offered sincere ignorance.

"Choose one," he said and looked at the nude slaves. His tone was soft, almost serene, innocent in that it offered no warning of what he was about to do; what he was about show her, show the prince, show them all.

Ibo frowned, unsure of why he wanted her to select from the chattel that stood before her. She watched Amir and did her best to mimic him, standing tall and proud, chest out, chin up, unfazed and untroubled by the horror that surrounded them.

"If you don't choose one," Rutgers continued, "I'll choose one for you."

When Ibo stood there quietly looking into his eyes, quiescent, resisting his authority, Rutgers walked over to the tallest, thickest man in the group in an angry hurry. Roughly, he forced the man over to the ship's mainmast, where a couple of crewmen locked both his wrists into restraints made of metal hoops above his head.

"Mr. Whitaker!" Rutgers called out.

"Sir!" Whitaker said in response, standing at attention, chest out, shoulders back.

"Mr. Whitaker, I don't think my guest understands the gravity or the sheer hopelessness of the situation." He grabbed a black bullwhip from the foremast and handed it to Whitaker. "Explain it to her. Make sure she gets all the details. Do you understand me, Mr. Whitaker?"

"Aye, Captain," Whitaker shouted, offered a quick,

rigid salute. "With pleasure, sir! Somebody's gotta teach these darkies how things are."

He took the whip from Rutgers and walked over to the man shackled to the mainmast. A delightful sneer emerged before he said, "You don't understand a word I'm sayin', do ya, nigger?" He paused and waited for a response, his eyes glaring into his victim's.

The man looked at Whitaker with eyes full of fury; eyes that bridged the communication gap; eyes that told his captor that if the opportunity ever presented itself, he wouldn't hesitate to rotate his head one hundred and eighty degrees, snapping his neck. And if it were possible, rotate it another one hundred and eighty degrees so that the circle would be complete.

Whitaker's tobacco-stained teeth slowly appeared as the corners of his mouth turned upward. Softly, he whispered in his ear, "You may not understand my words, but you do understand me, don't you? My best friend . . . Charlie . . . is dead because of you savages."

A single tear rolled down his cheek. He wiped it quickly before anyone other than the slave saw it.

"I loved Charlie," he continued, still whispering. "We been friends for near 'bout twenty years. Somebody gotta pay for him dyin' the way he did. The cap'em won't let me kill the prince, but I sho' as hell can kill you, nigger. And that's what I aim tuh do." He raised the whip to eye level. "I'm gonna peel you like a potato. Ya hear me? A potato!" And with that, he marked off the appropriate distance needed and looked at Captain Rutgers. "Ready, Cap'em."

Rutgers looked at Ibo and said, "You're about to enter a world where your life has little to no value. As a matter of fact, from now on, your life is in the hands of your owner. For the time being, that's me. Telling you that fact is not going to make you understand it, so Mr. Whitaker is going to make what I just said very clear." He paused briefly. "Tell the prince what I just said."

Ibo didn't move, didn't utter a sound; didn't even bat an eye. She just stared at Rutgers defiantly, like she was still in Nigeria, still on her father's farm, still safe from all things dangerous and all things that offend.

"Mr. Whitaker," Rutgers began, "you may commence."

Whitaker said, "Ya hear that, nigger? Ol' Cap'em here just gimme the okay to peel the skin off'n you."

Whoo! Whoo! Whoo!

Chapter 13

"Mr. Whitaker, toss the girl over the side."

A loud gasp filled the air when the whip connected to bare black flesh and pulled away several layers of skin, immediately followed by a bloodcurdling scream emitted by the man being whipped. It startled them when they heard the power of it. The scream was almost synchronous with the sound that crackled in the ears of terrified onlookers. Blood splashed across the children's faces that stood closest to the slave being lashed. It was important that the children more than the adults see the savagery, as it would forever alter their desire to defy their owners.

Sweat dripped from Mr. Whitaker's forehead as he delivered lash after merciless lash, enjoying every bit of the punishment he doled out. He saw nothing wrong with what he was doing. This was justice; justice for his lifelong friend Charlie. The black savages were animals and could be treated as such without remorse. Only a weak man felt sorry for the animal he killed. It was a matter of survival; survival of the fittest.

Although he enjoyed lashing the slave who had nothing to do with his friend's death, he was tiring. Nevertheless, his anger gave him the strength to continue for more than an hour.

Rutgers noticed that the slave's legs were no longer holding him up and he no longer cried out. "Enough!" he commanded.

"Ah, just a few more, Cap'em," Mr. Whitaker pleaded. "It's only right that these darkies see that they can't kill a white man and get away with it."

"I said enough!" Rutgers shouted. "He's lost consciousness."

Mr. Whitaker walked over to the man and kicked him. "Wake up, nigger!"

The man didn't move.

Mr. Whitaker kneeled down and checked him closer and then stood up and looked at Rutgers. "He's dead. And it serves him right. Charlie's dead; now he's dead. That's makes us almost even. A few more niggers gotta die to even the score. Otherwise, it would appear that one of their lives is the same as ours. The good Lord up above wouldn't like it if we took life for life with these darkies. He just wouldn't stand for it."

Rutgers looked at Ibo and said, "Explain it to the prince."

Ibo looked at Amir. He was still standing tall, unmoved by what he had seen, knowing that his strength, his indomitable spirit was being transferred to her vicariously. He quickly assessed the situation. Even though he did not understand the language the Dutchmen spoke, his eyes told him everything he needed to know. This was a chess match of epic proportions, and the lives of everyone on the ship, including the Dutchmen, hung in the balance. The captain was trying to use his love for Ibo to break his will to survive. If he allowed himself to be broken, they would all be broken. He, therefore, knew he had to model the role he wanted her to play.

Even though seeing a man beaten into submission and then beaten to death rocked her to the core of her existence, she shook her head, refusing to cooperate. If Amir could take it, so could she—at least that's what she told herself. But deep down, she wanted to beg Amir to cooperate. She felt as if the man was dead because she refused to show weakness; refused to compromise with those who would take their God-given freedom as if it were hewn out gold, stick it in flames to melt it down, and then shape it into whatever form they saw fit.

One of the crewmen shouted, "Man-eaters on the port bow, Cap'em."

Rutgers looked at Ibo. "Remember the sharks I told you about in my cabin?"

Ibo locked eyes with him defiantly.

"You're about to get a bird's eye view of what these man-eaters can do to a man in a matter of seconds." He looked at Mr. Whitaker. "Move them over to the port bow so they can see."

"Yes, sir, Cap'em," Whitaker said, smiling from ear to ear. "This'll scare the livin' daylights outta 'em."

Moments later, all the slaves were watching ten sharks swimming in a perpetual circle, waiting for their meal.

Rutgers grabbed Ibo by the arm and dragged her over to the side of the ship. "Look in the water!" He paused for a second when she looked in. "Don't make me do this! Tell the prince what I said!"

Ibo looked in the water. She saw the sharks, but was unafraid of what their powerful jaws could do. She had never seen them or their handiwork.

She looked at Rutgers and said, "No."

Rutgers sighed heavily. "You heard her, Mr. Whitaker."

A few seconds later, they tossed the dead slave in the Atlantic. They heard a loud splash. Water leapt out of the ocean when the dead slave crashed into it. Rapidly, the sharks swam to the slave. Those onboard learned first-hand what a man-eater was and what its powerful jaws were capable of. The sharks ripped into the slave's flesh and bone violently and incredibly swiftly. The slaves could hear the dead man's bones breaking. The sight of it was so surreal that many fainted; stomachs emptied. The children wailed loudly without the benefit of consolation.

"Decide!" Rutgers shouted again. However, this time, when he looked into her eyes, he could see that the sight of a man being eaten had lessened her resolve.

Ibo looked at the Prince. He was still unmoved, undaunted.

"No," she said, almost whispering; her tone without resolve, her fortitude, a memory.

Rutgers shook his head. "I don't get any pleasure out of this! Just tell the prince what I said and I'll end it here, now!"

Two tears climbed Ibo's high cheekbones, then raced down her tight jaw line and fell on the bloodied deck. Her resilience was nearly gone; it was about to spread it wings like an eagle and fly far away. She found a morsel of strength and shook her head in a final act of diminished defiance.

Rutgers shook his head and sighed heavily. This time he chose a woman. She was beaten to within an inch of her life and tossed to the sharks alive. Again they heard the sound of bones breaking. Again they heard wailing; a sound so full of emotion that it seized Ibo's heart and threatened to confiscate it. Two more tears raced down her fallen countenance. Nevertheless, after seeing Amir's strength, she refused a third time.

This time Rutgers chose a child—a girl no more than six years old. He chose her because she was one of the few children who had been captured in the field with her mother and father. When the father attempted to protect his daughter, he was shot and tossed to the sharks alive— bones broke, blood filled the sea.

This time Ibo didn't look at the prince. This time she made her own decision. This time she was going to save the little black girl's life. She walked over to the prince and said what Captain Rutgers had ordered her to say: "You're about to enter a world where your life has little to no value."

Chapter 14

Love Your Neighbor?

The prince turned his back to Ibo, angry with her because she had shown weakness and had given in to her emotions. He thought it better that they all die rather than become chattel, rather than become the animals the Dutchmen thought they were. Death was preferable to becoming complicit in their demise. Yet he wasn't without compassion for those who died such horrible deaths.

Compassion notwithstanding, he had to be strong for the men who studied his every move, his every emotion, because he would need them if and when the time came to turn the tables on their oppressors. He therefore had to be strong, only giving in when necessary; and only then as an act of retreat, never surrender. Even though he loved Ibo, the men had to see that even she took a backseat to strength and the need to survive. Strength was important for morale, and morale was a necessary ingredient for motivation, particularly when it came to battle.

When Captain Rutgers saw that, he said, "Mr. Whitaker!"

Whitaker snapped to attention. "Sir!"

Rutgers stared at Amir for a long second and then said, "Toss the girl over the side."

The girl's mother screamed and ran at the captain, but her chains retrained her. The girl knew what was about to happen to her and she resisted, clawing, biting, kicking. But being a child, she was no match for Whitaker, who tossed the girl to the sharks—bones broke, blood filled the ocean.

Seeing all the blood, hearing father and daughter cry out as they were being devoured took all the fight out of the slaves. They fell to their knees and wept unceasingly.

Amir saw their defeat and surrendered; bowing his head, he listened as Ibo translated Rutgers' words. When she finished, he nodded. From that moment forward, there would be no more rebellion, no more whippings, no more death.

Captain Rutgers had successfully separated the men from the women, the children from the parents, and most importantly, Ibo from the prince. And it would remain that way for the remainder of the voyage. For many it would remain that way for the rest of their very lives.

"By what authority do you do these things?" Amir said to Ibo.

She looked at Rutgers and translated Amir's words.

Rutgers smiled and pulled a small Bible from his vest and shook it in his face. "I do these things by the authority of the Lord Jesus Christ. This is the good book, and it says you were born to serve us, to be our slaves."

Ibo translated.

Amir looked Rutgers in the eyes. "If that were so, why do you force us? And why do we resist?"

Ibo translated.

"Because you're too ignorant to know that you are a cursed people. You've got the curse of Ham on you! All of you!"

Ibo translated.

"Too ignorant? Have you actually read the book you hold?"

Ibo translated.

Stunned by the questions, Rutgers stared at Amir, studying him for a moment or two. Even though he was a born again Christian and carried a Bible, he had never read it. Sure, he had read passages from the book of Psalms, Genesis, Proverbs, and the Gospels, but he had never actually read the Bible from cover to cover. His knowledge of it was incredibly limited. To be challenged by the prince, who could quite possibly be more knowledgeable than he, could not be tolerated; especially not in front of the Windward crew.

"Mr. Whitaker!" Rutgers called out.

Whitaker came to attention. "Sir!"

Still staring at Amir, he yelled angrily, "Take these *animals* back to their stalls and lock 'em up!"

Amir remembered the Bible lessons and the verses his mother, who converted from Islam to Christianity, had made him memorize. The verse seemed to come from someplace deep within, a place he no longer visited, but it was now apropos.

His eyes blazed with confidence when he looked at Rutgers' countenance and spoke in a tone that was even, reflective, and without malice.

Rutgers looked at Ibo, expecting her to translate what he had said.

Dumbfounded, she frowned and said, "I'm not sure what he meant, but he said, 'Mark 12:30 and 31.'"

Rutgers huffed a little when he learned what Amir had said. Nevertheless, he opened the Bible he was holding, turned to the selected passage, and read the following:

And you shall love the LORD your God with all your heart, with all your soul, with all your mind, and with all your strength. This is the first commandment. And the second, like it, is this: You shall love your neighbor as yourself.

There is no other commandment greater than these.

Ibo watched him as he read the passages and noticed that after reading them, he grew angry. Curious, she said, "What does it say?"

Rutgers slammed the Bible shut so roughly that it made a loud thud. Then he glared at her and said, "It says wives are to obey their husbands. That's what it says."

"Hmmm."

Hmpf! Why would he tell you to read that when you were talking about our lives being of little value?

Chapter 15

"Undress!"

It took three months to cross the Atlantic. The long voyage with no white women aboard made the African females very desirable. Three months at sea had a way of producing a level of debauchery in sailors few people experienced or even knew about. Raping the slave women was viewed as a perk for being a valued member of the crew.

Prior to reaching the coast of Africa, the crew of the Windward spoke daily of when they would be able to satisfy their burgeoning lust by ravaging young black virgins every night on the way to Santo Domingo, where they would unload a portion of the slaves and take on sugar, rum, and tobacco. Having cowed the prince, who was a threat to lead a successful rebellion, Captain Rutgers and his crew were ready to take the spoils of slavery without fear of being murdered in their sleep.

Rutgers grabbed Ibo by the arm and dragged her

below deck. He looked back over his shoulder and smiled at Amir, who was beside himself with rage. Below deck now, he dragged her down the narrow passageway that led to his cabin, and threw her on the floor.

After witnessing the depth of his cruelty on deck, she expected to be raped. She had no fight left in her. At sixteen, she had seen much more than she ever cared to. She thought about her mother and her father and how much better it would have been if she had just stayed at home the night she ran away to be with the love of her young and impressionable life.

Just as she was being dragged into the captain's cabin, she remembered Adesola, the man she was engaged to and the succeeding king of Dahomey, and how she had betrayed him with his brother. She wondered how much better off she would have been if she had married him like her father had planned. She further wondered what her mother thought of her betrayal. Did she think her a whore? By now they had to know that she and Amir had run off together.

"Undress!" she heard Rutgers shout.

Chapter 16

"I am a maiden. Please . . . don't deal with me in this manner."

Ibo sat there, still on the floor, looking up at him, thinking that she was about to be ruined for Amir, whom she still loved, but whom she blamed exclusively for all of this. He had promised her she would be happy and that they would have lots of children, and that he would be a builder of ships. Just the opposite had happened. They were not happy, they were not married, and if she had any children, it looked as if they would be Captain Rutgers' brood. When she thought of it all, she covered her face with her hands and wept uncontrollably.

Rutgers grabbed her by the shoulders and stood her up. He smelled the vomit on her purple silk and turned away when the stench registered in his mind. "Undress! Now!"

Whimpering, she said, "I am a maiden. Please . . . do not deal with me in this manner. I will do anything you say

. . . only do not do this dastardly deed. It will be a sin on your eternal soul."

Rutgers backhanded her and she fell backward onto the bed. "I said get undressed, girl! I'll be back in a few minutes and you better be butt naked when I return. If not, I'll toss the prince over the side and let the sharks eat him alive." He turned around and stormed out.

Rutgers returned a few minutes later with a naked black female at his side. With a fistful of her hair, he bent her over as he forced her into his cabin. It was clear that the young woman had been beaten; her cheek bones were swollen and bruised. Tears flowed freely. She kept pleading with Rutgers in her native language, but he had no idea what she was saying, nor did he care. She was his to do with as he pleased. Her desire for sex was not a prerequisite.

When he saw that Ibo was still fully dressed, he backhanded her again with his free hand. She fell to the floor. Still using the other woman's hair to control her, he threw her onto the bed.

Trembling, the woman watched to see what he would do to the woman already in the room when they arrived. She hoped that he would choose her instead. If Rutgers was going to violate one of them, she didn't want it to be her.

He grabbed Ibo by the shoulders and stood her up. Then he slapped her again.

She felt her warm blood run down both nostrils, over her lips, down her chin, and onto her soiled clothing. Dazed and disoriented, she heard the tearing of clothing. A second or so later, she realized Rutgers had torn her expensive frock down the middle and her bare breasts were exposed and bouncing. She tried to fight him off, but he slapped her again.

When she could focus again, she was sitting in a velvet-lined spoon-back chair. She could see Captain Rutgers raping the female he had brought with him. She was lying on her stomach and Rutgers was on top of her—thrusting wildly, violently. But a strange thing was happening. He was watching Ibo the entire time. Looking into her deep-set brown eyes drove him wild. Her full lips made him want to take them into his mouth and gently kiss and suckle them.

He continued staring; thrusting powerfully, ignoring the woman's pain-filled cries as if he couldn't hear them. But he could hear them. Her cries were a part of it. They added to his pleasure. The more the woman cried and pleaded, the better it felt to him. With each thrust, his gaze seemed to intensify.

That's when Ibo realized that the woman he was raping was a substitute for what he wanted to do to her. She looked at the woman.

They locked eyes.

The woman's eyes begged for help, but Ibo didn't move, couldn't move. What she saw was a horrifying spectacle of depravity, and yet she couldn't stop watching the atrocity.

She looked into Rutgers' eyes again. She could tell he was enjoying the sex he took by force, because his eyes had rolled back into his head. She could barely see his pupils.

Rutgers regained focus and locked eyes with Ibo until

he finished, until all of his intensity left him and entered the girl, until his entire body relaxed, until his eyes became drowsy, and he fell asleep on top of the girl. She was still sobbing quietly into the fabric of the polychromatic quilt that covered the bed.

Chapter 17

"Oh, my darling. Oh, my love, please answer me."

Ibo waited until she was sure Rutgers was in a deep sleep before allowing herself to move an inch, watching him and the girl for nearly forty-five minutes without so much as batting her eyelashes. During that time, Rutgers had moved only slightly and made a few night sounds, which made her even more cautious. The girl appeared to be sleeping too.

Finally, she forced herself to get up from the chair that had turned her into a voyeur of the wickedly violent seizure. Still naked, she crept over to the trunk that contained her clothing and opened it.

All of her clothes were still neatly folded and pristine. She found another garment to wear; this one wasn't as classy or stately as the other and not nearly as pretty. Earlier that day, she had given a lot of thought as to what she would wear when she saw Amir. She had wanted to make the right statement, even in custody, believing that it was temporary, believing their marriage would be permanent. Therefore, she had been quite meticulous in selecting just the right dress so that she would at least be presentable in the presence of the prince.

Purple was the color of royalty, and she had wanted the prince to know that even in captivity, she was worthy to be his wife. On their three-day journey, she had told the prince that of all the garments his mother had made for her, she loved that particular piece best. When she put it on, she thought it would please him. She wanted to be beautiful and desirable so that when they were free again, he would still want her. But now, after having shown her humanness, after being weak and throwing up the contents of her stomach in front of foreigners, she felt as if she had lost a measure of respect in his eyes. Giving in to Captain Rutgers' demands had made matters worse.

She had noticed that the man who had been guarding her was no longer there when Rutgers brought the woman back to the cabin. She assumed he was above deck with the rest of the Dutchmen.

She had to find Amir. She had to find out what they were going to do to get out of the mess they found themselves in. Amir would have a plan, she knew, or at least believed. Even though she blamed him for everything, she knew that if they had any chance of being free again, he would have to be liberated. If he could emancipate them somehow and return them to the shores of their native land, all would be forgiven and their capture would be a distant but unforgettable narrative that they would pass down from generation to generation.

At the cabin door now, she looked back at Rutgers to

see if he and the girl were still asleep. With her body still facing the door, she swiveled her head to the right, peering over her slender shoulder. Rutgers was still in a deep sleep, but the girl was watching Ibo's every move while his heavy weight nearly smothered her.

Although the woman never said a word, her eyes pleaded for Ibo to escape and come back and free her. Her eyes screamed for justice for what he had done to her, what he had done to them all that day. Her eyes were full of murderous revenge—sweet and extremely cold. For those reasons, Ibo knew she would remain perfectly still, perfectly quiet until she returned. They were in this together.

Carefully, she turned the knob and pulled back the door. With it open, she looked for the guard. She didn't see him in the passageway. She looked back again. Rutgers didn't move. The girl's eyes encouraged her to go and free the others so that they could kill the white men that had done this evil to them. She slipped out the door and then pulled it behind her, leaving it partially open, not making a sound. Her heart thundered, *ba-boom, ba-boom, ba-boom,* feeling like it would burst and end her life at any moment.

She quelled her fear and made her way down the torch-lit corridor, hearing groans of ecstasy and moans of misery. Loud slaps penetrated the walls, followed immediately by agonizing pleas for mercy. Brutal violations were taking place behind every door she passed. The cries of the women were so piercing that she knew she would never forget those sounds. She wanted to open the doors and help them subdue the Dutchmen, but knew she had to keep moving, she had to stay focused; first things first—she was safe as long as the men were "entertaining" themselves.

As she neared the end of the passageway, she saw stairs that led to the deck. Another set of stairs went farther into the bowels of the ship. She heard a couple of Dutchmen talking at the top of the stairs. She couldn't quite make out what they were saying, as they were too far away.

Hoping they wouldn't hear her, she made her way down to the cargo hold, where she hoped to find Amir and the other hostages. As she descended farther and farther into the recesses of the Windward, she could feel the unrelenting heat rising, as if it were coming from a great furnace. Before long, she could hear groans of despair and motion sickness. And then the foul air hit her bloodied nose with the force of a sledgehammer and threatened to knock her out, but she marched on, kept moving ever downward into the pit that could be aptly described as hell on water.

Guided by a crescendo of groans, she approached the end of her furtive journey, but she was impeded by a final door. She turned the knob and pushed, but the door was locked. With her hands, she searched for a way to unlock it. Having found the way in, she slid the bar to the right and turned the knob again. The door opened, and the smell that came from that place rocked her equilibrium and forced her to her knees, where she vomited a second time. She wasn't alone, though. She could hear dozens of others throwing up too.

Still on her knees, she called out to him. Her voice trembled when she spoke his name. "Amir. My sweet

Amir." Hearing nothing, she called out again, her voice still quivering, "Oh, my darling. Oh, my love, please answer me." Overcome by emotion, she called out a third time, "Guide me to your side and I will free you."

Like a mother who can distinguish her infant's cry from all others, her ears, like radar, locked in on the only voice that mattered at that moment.

"Ibo," he called out. His voice was strong and commanding. "I am here. Come to me."

Chapter 18

"I promise you I will come for you."

Amir's voice was like an oasis in a dry and barren place. It watered her dry heart, which ached for only him, and reinvigorated her strength of mind. On her hands and knees, she crawled to the voice that led her through the dimly-lit dungeon. On the way, her eyes took in the horrors of slavery. She saw hundreds of men, row upon row of them, shackled together, packed like sardines. She heaved a couple more times, but managed to control the urge to spill her insides on the floor.

Rutgers had shielded her from it, as she was a pearl of great price. She had been fed regular food and kept in mint condition so that she would bring him maximum price. But there, in the hellish belly of the Windward, she knew for the second time what it meant to be owned by Dutchmen. There, in that dark and filthy place, where men were chained together, she recognized and even felt a level of gloom that if embraced, undermined hope's audacity.

"I am here," his voice called out again.

She looked to the left and there was Amir, chained to two men, one on the left and the other on the right. She cringed when her eyes beheld him. His royal highness was on his back, completely nude, lying in his own filth. Vomit was on his face and at the corners of what was once a regal mouth. She couldn't distinguish his vile smell from that of his shackled brothers, one of whom was dead and beginning to rot.

Seeing Amir in that state robbed her of a certain measure of respect that she once had for him. Seeing him in that state knocked him off the throne she had put him on. Seeing him in that state awakened her to a reality never before imagined, and she lost heart. How was he going to save her when he couldn't even save himself?

Amir turned his head to the left and vomited on the dead man. He turned to her again and said, "You must be strong if you are to survive."

When his vile breath entered her nose, she nearly fainted. Were she not already on her knees, she would have been. She forced herself to stop breathing so she could concentrate on his words.

"Do you understand, Ibo? You must be strong."

No longer able to restrain them, the tears flowed freely and she wept aloud. "I understand, but I came to free you and the others!"

"No. The time is not right."

"But, Amir, the Dutchmen are forcing us! They are taking the things most sacred. Do you not care?"

Amir ignored her question. Of course he cared, of course he wanted to be free, of course he wanted to take all their heads off at the shoulders.

With compassion, he said, "I know, my love. But you will survive even that, and we will have our revenge on the Dutchmen."

"But, Amir, Captain Rutgers raped a woman right in front of me. He made me watch with no clothes to cover me."

"You must pretend to cooperate, but your heart will be as a ravenous lion. Your tongue must become a wily serpent. And then, when they least expect it, we will come out of the shadows and crush them. We will do what they have done to us—everything they have done, we will do in like manner. We will take no prisoners; we will leave none of them alive—their families too. They must all die swiftly and without mercy.

"Use whatever happens to you to make you strong, and then you will be able to destroy your enemy. Do everything you can to make him feel safe and he will relax. Make him think you have accepted him as your lord. Can you do that, my love?"

"I don't know, Amir. What if he wants me? What then?"

"If he was going to force you, he would have by now. But . . . if it happens, use even that to weaken him. Can you do that?"

"Oh, Amir, I don't know. I don't know if I can do that. I would rather die than give the Dutchmen the thing most sacred."

"I don't want this for you, my love. Survival is first. Revenge second. There can be no revenge without survival;

therefore, you must, Ibo. Now, leave this place before you are discovered."

"What about you, Amir? Will you survive in this dark and filthy place?"

"I will. My resolve is strong. I have made up my mind. I will not be broken. Now . . . leave this place and do not come back. Be ready at all times. An opportunity will present itself at the right moment. Be patient."

Weakly, she said, "Okay."

"Let me hear you say you will do whatever it takes to survive."

She bowed her head and whispered, "I'll do whatever it takes to survive."

"Louder!"

Firmly, she said, "I'll do whatever it takes to survive."

"Say it like you believe it, Ibo! Say it with conviction!"

"I'll do whatever it takes to survive!"

"Keep saying it until you believe it, and you will survive. Be patient for as long as it takes. I will be with you in spirit. I promise you I will come for you."

Chapter 19

"Grant me this request, Lord God of Israel."

When Amir heard the door shut and the bar slide across, locking them in for the night, the conversation he'd had with his mother prior to leaving came to mind. She had told him that she prayed to the Lord God of Israel that he would be with Amir on his journey. She had said, "The Lord God doesn't guarantee you a life without trouble. He only promises to be with you and never leave you through whatever trouble comes your way. Trust him, my son."

He closed his eyes and soon he was there, back with his mother, in their home. When he thought of her, he remembered that she had sacrificed her life for them. Tears filled his eyes and spilled out of the corners.

Amidst all the groans and agony that filled the prison he was in, he wept for his mother, who, he believed, had died a painful death for nothing. His mother had been good to him. She had taught him what real love was by sacrificing herself so that he could have the happiness she never had. The thing that bothered him most was that she didn't hesitate to die so that he could live; so that he could pursue the thing that he thought would bring him the most happiness—Ibo Atikah Mustafa. But because he was careless, because he relaxed and allowed himself the luxury of a deep, satisfying sleep, her sacrifice was in vain.

As the Windward journeyed on, moving farther and farther away from the coast of Africa, memories of his betrayal washed over him like a great tidal wave. He remembered his brother's jubilant smile when he spoke of Ibo and his upcoming marriage. Adesola had called a great feast to celebrate and had invited all of his brothers. Amir attended the feast and had eaten with his brother, knowing he was going to take his bride and make her his own. He knew what he was doing was wrong, but the thing had gone too far. He had fallen for Ibo, and she for him.

He told himself that Adesola had other wives and that he didn't need another; especially one he didn't love and one who did not love him. Now, looking back on it, Amir was sorry for what he had done, wishing he could stop time and reverse it so that he and Ibo wouldn't be on a Dutch ship; so that his beloved mother would not have died in vain. But it was too late. Time stood still for no man, and what he set into motion would have to play itself out to the very end.

Even though he told Ibo to be strong and to survive, he didn't believe it himself. He realized that he had been stripped of everything, that he was powerless, that neither muscle nor pride would save him from the plight before him. That's when he thought about his mother's God and called upon him in his desperation.

With his eyes closed, he opened his mouth and spoke thusly: "Oh Lord God of my mother . . . hear me. Hear my prayer. From my youth I have heard of you from my mother's voice. She has read me many wonderful things about you. She has told me of your mighty power . . . your great wisdom . . . and your everlasting mercy. I do not know if I ever believed in you, but I know she did. I pray to you, if you exist, and I ask that you grant me my freedom and the power to take vengeance on the Dutchmen who brought me to this place.

"I know I have given you no reason to grant me such a request. I do not even expect you to do this thing for my sake. I ask that you do this thing for my mother's sake. It was she who told me you would be with me in times like this. I pray, therefore, that you honor my mother as she honored your word.

"Grant me this request, Lord God of Israel. Grant me this request and I will believe in you for the rest of my life. Free me and give me the power to make my enemies pay for what they have done to me, and I will give you my life."

When he finished his prayer, a great calm came over him and he drifted off to sleep.

Chapter 20

"I don't care what the other white men do as long as I kill this one."

Standing outside of the cargo hold, Ibo was conflicted when she left Amir in that awful place. She wanted freedom now; she wanted revenge now. However, in her heart, she knew Amir was right. Even though they vastly outnumbered the Windward crew, the men in the cargo hold were far too weak to overthrow them. It looked as if many of them were knocking on the door of death, waiting for it to open.

She locked the door and made her way back up the stairs where cool, fresh air lived. The passageway leading to Captain Rutgers' cabin was quiet now, as if everyone had fallen asleep.

Quietly, she crept down the corridor leading to Rutgers' quarters. Having reached the partially open door, she slowly pushed it open. Rutgers was still fast asleep, still on top of the girl he had raped. The girl's eyes offered confusion. Then she frowned. Ibo knew she was wondering why she hadn't brought help. She put her index finger to her lips, hoping the woman wouldn't speak.

Rutgers grunted and rolled off the woman and onto his back.

Both women froze. They were so afraid of him waking up that they didn't dare breath.

The girl continued staring at Ibo, wondering if Rutgers had opened his eyes and saw that she was no longer in the chair. Ibo's index finger was still at her lips. Then she raised both her palms to the girl, letting her know he was still sleeping.

When the girl heard Rutgers snore, her face contorted. Then she whispered, "What happened?"

"The prince says to wait."

"Wait? For what?" the woman screamed a whisper. "For them to kill us all? To be thrown in the water and be eaten alive? To be forced again and again? Is this what we wait for?"

With strong resolve, Ibo screamed a whisper of her own. "If necessary, yes!"

"That's easy for you to say! You just sit there and watch! You don't have to worry about the white man forcing himself inside you like the rest of us!"

"Not now, no. But later, I'm afraid we will all suffer the same fate. We must stick together, or we will all die one by one."

The woman swiveled her head to the left and looked at Rutgers. He was still asleep. She eased off the bed and started looking around.

"What are you doing?" Ibo asked. "Lay back down before he wakes up."

"No. I will kill him now. While he sleeps."

"Wait. If you kill him, what will the other white men do?"

"I don't care what the other white men do as long as I kill this one."

The girl slid open a drawer, looking for a knife to plunge into his heart. Finding nothing, she eased open another and another, only to be disappointed again and again. Then she looked under the bed and found a case. She grabbed and opened it and discovered that it held the firearm that she had seen him use.

When she stood up, a triumphant frown covered her face; a look of murderous rapture sprang forth. She pointed the gun in Rutgers' face, right under his nose, determined to blow it clean off.

Ibo grabbed her arm just before the weapon discharged. *Ka-boom!*

Sulfur filled the air.

A very naked Captain Rutgers woke up and saw the two girls struggling over the gun. When the woman realized that he had awakened, she dropped the gun, broke away from Ibo, and ran through the open cabin door. Rutgers grabbed his pants, slid into them as quickly as he could, and ran after her. Ibo stayed behind them and watched from the open doorway.

Chapter 21

Someone was about to die.

Ibo watched Rutgers run down the passageway, chasing the girl who had tried to kill him. The other officers came out of their cabins, shirtless, with their weapons drawn and pointed toward the ceiling. They were puzzled by the gunshot that woke them all. Suddenly, the corridor was filled with naked, hysterical women, screaming and running, trying to escape the men who had plundered them.

Rutgers told his men what had happened. He told some of the men to guard the cargo hold. They ran in haste down the stairs. The rest of the officers ran after the girl, who was on her way up the stairs to the deck. Evil covered their faces.

It was then that Ibo began to second guess herself. Standing there in the doorway, she began to wonder if she had done the right thing. Then she realized that if she had let the woman kill Rutgers, another officer would have surely taken over and he, given what was happening to all the women, would have forced her that very night.

On the other hand, she realized that by saving Rutgers' life, she had doomed the girl to death. They were going to catch her, she knew. There was no doubt about that. They were aboard a ship at sea. How far could she run? Where could she hide and for how long?

The Windward crew was going to be alert for the rest of the voyage. Security would be tighter. Freeing Amir was going to be nearly impossible now. She wished she hadn't denied the girl the satisfaction of killing Rutgers before her rendezvous with the grim reaper. If she had, at least one of the Dutchmen would be dead.

Then it occurred to her that saving Rutgers' life could play into her hands the way Amir had planned. She realized that even if he never acknowledged it, she had saved his life, and if he was any kind of man, if he was any kind of human being, he would be in her debt for as long as he lived.

When she realized this, she no longer worried about the fate of the girl, who would die any moment now. Besides, she rationalized that the girl preferred death to being raped every night. She had said as much herself. Saving Rutgers' life gave the girl what she wanted—death and the freedom that came with it.

Quickly, she left the cabin and made her way down the empty passageway. She climbed the stairs and went on deck. She had to see what was going to happen. She had to know how it would end for the girl who, without realizing it, had given Ibo the advantage she would need to repay those who had destroyed her romantic dream.

The darkness on deck was so thick she could feel it. It was so dark that she couldn't see her hand in front of her face. The officers lit torches. The crackling flame sliced into the night. The women were still screaming, still running around with nowhere to go but into the sea. Several of them jumped overboard, preferring a watery grave to becoming a bed wench and producing children who would be condemned to the same the moment they heard themselves cry.

She heard loud splashes along with ear-piercing screams as they plunged into the Atlantic. She saw Mr. Whitaker on the starboard side of the ship, using a torch as he looked around for the girl who had tried to kill Captain Rutgers. All of a sudden, the woman came out of the darkness and ran toward him at full speed from the other side of the ship. Mr. Whitaker didn't see her.

The woman hit him with enough force to take them both over the side. Two loud splashes filled the night. When Ibo saw it, a satisfied smile bubbled to the surface and remained.

Happy that she and the woman had both gotten a measure of revenge, she returned to the cabin. She covered her mouth so that her laughter would not be heard.

Chapter 22

"Am I to assume you will grant me anything but my freedom then?"

A couple of hours later, she heard the cabin door open and close. After searching fruitlessly for the key that would unlock the chains that secured Amir and the other men, she had fallen asleep in the lavender velvet spoonback chair. She opened her eyes. Captain Rutgers was staring at her. For a few unsettling moments, they just looked at each other, neither of them saying a word; both of them contemplating what had happened and what would happen next.

On the way back to his cabin, Rutgers thought about what had happened and knew he was lucky to be alive. He had raped a woman and was brazen enough to fall asleep on top of her. He had also been careless in that he left a loaded weapon in a place where the woman could find it and blow his brains out. If one of his men had done that, he would have stripped him of his rank and flogged him.

Being the captain of a seafaring vessel, he knew he would have to set a much better example for his men.

The gun was still right where the woman had dropped it. He picked it up and looked at the instrument of death. He had used that very gun to kill a number of men. Most recently, one of his own who was about to shoot and kill Ibo Atikah Mustafa, the precious cargo that he had tried to procure from her father a number of times. The irony of her saving his life left him feeling totally indebted to her. Saving his life meant that anything he did, no matter how insignificant, would not have been possible were it not for her intervention.

He looked at Ibo again. She was still watching him. He got on his knees and looked under the bed. Then he grabbed the case that had been specially made for the weapon. He put the pistol in it and closed it again. The weapon had been discharged, so it could no longer be used to threaten his life. He slid it back under the bed.

He stood up and looked at Ibo again and said, "I suppose I owe you my life."

There was no change in her expression when she said, "I *suppose* I owe *you* my virginity."

Rutgers almost smiled when he heard her reply. "Tell me something," he said sincerely. "Why? Why would you save the life of a man who snatched you from your homeland?"

Ibo raise her left brow before saying, "Why would you snatch me from my land, yet allow me to have my clothing, eat the same food you eat, and not do to me what you did to the girl I saved you from? And why were you staring at me while you . . . ?"

Rutgers sat down in one his chairs and ran his hand down his face and then fingered his beard. "One question at a time."

Ibo nodded.

"Now, why didn't you let her kill me, your captor?"

"Because if she had killed you, how would I know whether the man who replaced you wouldn't do to me what you refused to do? With you, I was safe. With another, I do not think I would be."

"So, self-preservation?"

"I do not understand the word *preservation*. What does it mean?"

"It is as you said—to be safe."

"Then yes, it is as you have said—self-preservation."

"I suppose you *think* I owe you something. Your *freedom*, perhaps?"

"You do owe me something, Captain Rutgers. You owe me your *life*. The only question now is how do you plan to pay your debt?"

"I've been thinking about that. I hate owing anybody anything, least of all my life. It makes people think they have something on you. That's why I always pay my debts! And I pay them on time! I make darn sure I owe no man anything, and I do everything I can to ensure that he owes me.

"Unfortunately, I do owe you my life, as you have said. So, tell me, what do you want?"

She wrinkled her forehead, stunned that he would ask her that. The question truly puzzled her because the answer was so obvious.

"What do I *want?*" she asked forcefully, on the verge of

yelling. "I want what every *hostage* on the ship wants. I want you to turn the ship around and take us all back home where we belong."

Rutgers laughed loud and hard. "Forget about it. That's never going to happen. You'll never see your home again. Get used to it. Stop thinking about it, because it'll never ever happen. Start thinking about building a new life in a new place—America. New Orleans, that's where you're going."

"And then you'll set us free?"

"Us?"

"The prince and me."

Rutgers stood up and paced the floor. Then he stopped and looked at her again. "You're so beautiful. You're worth more money to me than all the others combined. I cannot let you go without getting something for you. That's why I have taken good care of you, to answer your question. Your value will be high in New Orleans."

He quieted himself and thought for a few seconds. "How about this? Since I cannot let you go, I'll do everything I can to make sure that the man who buys you is the kind of man that will treat you well. How about that?"

"Do you have a family, Captain Rutgers?"

He shook his head.

"No wife?"

"No."

"I see."

After a long pause, Rutgers said, "You see what?"

"I see why you have no soul, sir. I see why you could do what you did to the girl you brought in here. I see why you can do what you did to us all. You can beat a man to death with a whip and toss him to the sharks. You can do the same to a woman and child because you have no soul, sir. You have no sense of family and the importance of it. You have no respect for others because you have no respect for yourself.

"I'm just wondering why you sold your soul. What happened to you? Who destroyed you? What could lead a man to do such things, and still be so deceived as to think that God is with you in such things?"

Rutgers found her words to be both penetrating and true, but he did his best to ignore her comments about his lack of a soul. He refused to let her see how on target she really was.

He remained stone-faced and said, "Here's what I'm prepared to do: I'll get a friend who I trust to buy the prince when we get to the Isle of Santo Domingo. There, the prince will have a chance to buy his freedom. You'll have the same chance for freedom in New Orleans. Now, it will take some years, but there is a chance that you and the prince can reunite. That's the best I can do."

"That not the best you can do, Captain Rutgers, and you know it. You can do a whole lot better than that."

"What would make us even then? And again, forget about your freedom. You're going to have to earn that yourself."

"Am I to assume that by saving your life you will grant me anything but my freedom then?"

Chapter 23

From Humanity to Commodity

Her question forced Rutgers to think deeply about his own convictions. He was in a difficult position; being the one who kidnapped and caged her, he now owed his very life to her. His conscience was pricked by her accurate commentary, but money was the deciding factor; it was an intoxicating influence. It stymied desirable virtues like veracity and personal integrity. It caused much conflict and consternation. He felt the need to alleviate his conscience and keep her as his private chattel at the same time.

After a few minutes passed, he smiled confidently, attempting to put her at ease. He said, "If it will square us, yes. I will give you anything but your freedom."

Ibo quieted her spirit and relaxed. She looked at his bookshelf. Then, as if she'd had an epiphany, she walked over to it and ran her fingers along the covers as she looked at the titles. She looked at row after row of thick books and wondered what usable information they contained. She had always being intelligent, contemplative, and insatiably hungry for knowledge.

Still looking at the rows of books, she asked, "What language do they speak in America?"

"English for the most part. But where you're going, there is a mixture of English, French, and Spanish; languages you already speak."

Still looking at the books, she said, "Yes, but I cannot read English or any of the others. I am able to pick up just about any language I hear. It is a gift from your God."

She paused and looked at him to see what his response would be to her reference of the divine. He smirked and kind of huffed. As far as she was concerned, there could be no doubt that any person who could pick up languages as easily as she could, must be endowed by a power greater than man.

"But I have never learned to read those same languages. I never had a teacher of those languages. If I had a willing teacher, I could learn to read and write in those languages. Then I might be able to free myself one day, as you say."

"Slaves are not supposed to read and write in America. Some masters would kill you for that. On the other hand, New Orleans is a different kind of place. Come to think of it, so is the Isle of Santo Domingo. Both have a generous population of free people of color who have become wealthy innovators. Who says you can't do the same if you want it badly enough?"

She went back over to the table and sat down. She laced her fingers together and looked him in the eyes. "The man you're going to sell me to . . . will he kill me even though I could be of benefit to him?"

"I don't think he will. I will let him know about your abilities and perhaps he can put them to good use."

She went back over to his bookshelf and fingered the books again, as if she were looking for just the right one. Although she couldn't read the words, she could tell that there was a series of books that seemed to have the same name on them. She picked up one of them and said, "What is this about?"

He walked over to where she was standing and took the book out of her hand. Still looking at the title, he said, "This is the works of William Shakespeare. There are several volumes."

"Tell me about them."

"It will take quite some time to tell you about his stories. The subject matter is vast and the depth is nearly bottomless. It is full of political intrigue, romance, sex, betrayal, and death. Are you sure you want to start with those?"

"Romance? Yes, and I want to start right now."

"Well, then, I suppose we should start with Romeo and Juliet. It seems so appropriate given the circumstances of your capture."

What Captain Rutgers didn't tell her was that the story of Romeo and Juliet was just as applicable to his life as it was to hers.

For the next three months, she read all of Shakespeare's plays and sonnets. She was particularly fond of his tragedies. Her favorite plays were *Antony and Cleopatra, Coriolanus, Julius Caesar, Othello,* and, of course, *Romeo and Juliet,* not necessarily in that order.

In *Antony and Cleopatra,* she admired Octavius' political cunning; in *Othello,* she admired Iago's diabolical deception; in *Coriolanus,* she admired Caius Martius' combative spirit; in *Julius Caesar,* she observed and reveled in the art of conspiracy; in *Romeo and Juliet,* she saw herself dealing with the bonds of love. All of these would be her mentors and become the weapons of a war she intended to wage once they reached the shores of someplace called New Orleans.

For three months, Rutgers and Ibo sat at his dining table and discussed the plays and what they meant. He found her essays on the works of William Shakespeare to be of unusual depth and delightfully trenchant. Rutgers watched her grow at an alarming rate and knew that she would be a dangerous foe for whoever stood in her way.

Over the months, during the course of their many conversations, he found it difficult not to fall in love with her. Her mind was sharp and engaging, her wit was intoxicating, and her beauty, which seemed to grow with each passing day, extraordinary. As much as he wanted to know her carnally, he couldn't, for two reasons.

First and foremost, she was a commodity. Her value had perhaps increased because of all that he had taught her. Being unblemished at the time of the auction would bring him a tidy sum. Second, he no longer saw her as he once did—a non-person. She had not only become sentient and real, she had become so much more. And as a real person, he could not violate her without further violating his conscience. He therefore satisfied his ever-growing lust for her with one of the other women, but never again in her presence.

Chapter 24

Wicked Betrayal

Captain Joseph Rutgers was born in 1742 on the west coast of Belgium in a town called Westland, which sat on the North Sea. He was the son of Pentecostal Evangelists—both he and his younger brother, Jonah, born a year later in 1743. They competed with each other constantly to see who could run the fastest, swim farther, or catch the most fish. When it came to competition, it didn't matter what the activity was; one had to show the other who was the best at it. This was especially true when it came to the affections of their mother. The competition for her attention was so intense that if she so much as smiled at one and not the other, a fistfight would ensue.

Joseph was obedient to a fault, doing whatever his mother and father told him to the letter. He was virtuous to the core of his being, tenderhearted and kind, particularly where women were concerned. Jonah, on the other hand, was the polar opposite of his older brother. He was a total rebel, a brawler and a lothario, having little to no respect for those of the female persuasion. He wore these attributes as if they were badges of honor.

The more obedient Joseph was the more defiant Jonah became. When Joseph committed his life to God, Jonah committed his life to wickedness. Through it all they loved each other fiercely, defending each other whenever the need arose, but only because they carried the same blood in their veins. Besides great fondness for their mother, the boys had one thing in common—an affinity for the sea.

Both men felt the call of the sea and became mariners together, traveling the known world, living carefree, with no responsibilities to tie them down. They had learned the ins and outs of sailing, and had become navigators. They had hoped to one day own their own ships or be captains.

Over the years, Joseph and Jonah became extremely close. Joseph became less rigid when it came to his religious beliefs, and Jonah wasn't as rebellious as he once was. All of that changed when they met and fell in love with a sexy blond Aussie named Tracy Combs at a fruit and vegetable market near the docks in Australia.

Tracy Combs had a bright, inviting smile that won them over in an instant. She was a sweet, shy, and well-behaved twenty-one-year-old Catholic woman when they met her. She was quite taken with both brothers and had difficulty deciding which one she wanted to spend the rest of her life with. She loved Joseph's innocence and sense of fair play, but she was drawn to Jonah's tough guy behavior and his naughty conversation.

When the time came to decide which brother she wanted, she chose Joseph because he could be trusted to never hurt her. Fidelity was a trait that Jonah simply did not have, and she didn't see him developing that virtue any time soon. Besides, she and Joseph had the same belief system. Although Jonah could quote Bible verses better than both of them, he never even acknowledged that there was a God. He was the ultimate skeptic.

What Tracy didn't count on was her own untrustworthiness, which was why, after marrying Joseph, she ended up in bed with Jonah. She thought herself to be virtuous and religiously chaste, a true believer in the Almighty and his son Jesus Christ. And she had been, up to the moment she met Jonah; she believed in God even as she peeled off her clothing and got into bed with him. He had awakened something in her; something vile and wicked. His words were like delicious sweet potato pie, and she ate every word like they were the last pieces she would ever have.

Over the course of time, she found her own wicked thoughts of her and Jonah doing the naughty things he suggested tantalizing, and stood at the precipice of embracing them. She was edging ever closer to the brilliant flame of wickedness, but she thought she could control herself. Fantasies of Jonah ruled her thoughts and dreams so much that one day she allowed Jonah to kiss her on the mouth. The kiss was so powerful and yet so sweet that it ignited a blaze in her private place and threatened to slowly melt her moral defenses as if they were candles. Day after day, her feelings for Jonah dominated her mind and grew more lewd each time she thought of him.

That's when she decided to marry Joseph, even

though his kisses left her feeling morally pure. But feeling morally pure was not exactly what she wanted. She wanted passion; the kind of passion that left one feeling out of control. She wanted to be driven to the edge of sex, to be inebriated by it, and then lose all power to resist its magnetic pull. Jonah offered her that incredible sensation and much more.

But when she saw Joseph watching them together thrusting wildly against each other, when she realized he heard them howling like werewolves, she knew the sight of it shattered his heart. Joseph had warned her many times about his brother, telling her what he was capable of. Now he knew what she was capable. Now he knew that she, too, harbored a wicked heart of deception.

Chapter 25

Can Beauty Resurrect the Dead?

When she saw him standing there like a statue, stunned and unmoving, with his mouth open at the horror of it all, staring at them while they made love in his bed, she came to her senses and realized that she had dishonored her husband and disgraced herself. More importantly, she had disgraced the God she still believed in even while she was in the midst of sinning against him. But it was too late—too late for apologies, too late for forgiveness, too late for any hope of reconciliation with Joseph. Suddenly, she lost the desire to continue the act and wanted Jonah to stop his powerful thrusts.

Jonah, on the other hand, had no idea Joseph was standing in the doorway watching it all. He was so into the moment that he couldn't stop if he wanted to. And so he continued the act until it was completed, even though she begged him to stop. If she had said stop once, she had said it a million times. She never meant it before, so he naturally thought she didn't mean it this time either. She didn't mean it when he kissed her. She didn't mean it when he caressed her covered breasts. She didn't mean it when he ripped open her blouse. She didn't mean it when he kissed and suckled her bare nipples. She didn't mean it when he put his hand up her dress and inside her panties. To all of this, she said stop weakly. No power. No conviction. When he didn't stop, but rather continued the acts she enjoyed, she consented with yet another weak "Stop," but it was more like an erotic sigh.

Initially, Joseph was in a mild state of shock. But when he came to himself, he realized what his brother had done to him. Murderous rage rose and threatened to consume him. After his brother had spilled his seed into his wife and was about to pull out of her, he grabbed a hunk of his thick black hair and pulled him the rest of the way out of his wife. Then he pounded his face with both fists until it was a bloody mess. Still full of rage, he choked his brother until he turned blue; until his eyes bulged out of his head. He would have continued choking him until he died, but Tracy pleaded with him to stop. He couldn't hear her because his anger muted the sound. He didn't let his brother go until he felt Tracy's laced fingers under his chin, pulling him away from Jonah.

After his dance with imminent death, Jonah became a devout Christian; more devout and more committed than Joseph ever was. He never touched Tracy again, and now had his own wife and children. He made it his life's mission to win his brother back to the church. He waited at the dock every time the Windward pulled in with hostages. He apologized to his brother and told him that what he was doing was sin in the sight of God.

The incident had occurred more than twenty years earlier, and still he had not successfully won his brother to God. He hadn't gotten him to speak to him or even look at him. Joseph walked past him as if he were an invisible man. But his words about the evils of slavery always left a perpetual dagger in Joseph's heart.

The wicked betrayal changed Joseph forever. It hardened him. He swore in his wrath that he would never love again. The love he had for his brother turned into bitter hatred. The burning hot love he had for Tracy melted like ice cream on a hot, muggy day. The love he had for his God turned cold because he blamed him for it all. He had been a good man for the better part of his life. He told himself he didn't deserve to be treated the way he had been treated. He told himself that it was better to do evil rather than good, and pursued it like it was cool water in a sweltering, desolate place.

As the years passed he became more bitter, not less. He decided to live by his own standards, which sunk him deeper into the abyss of resentment. He was miserable, and only felt a sense of peace on the sea. When an opportunity to take command of a slave ship was presented to him ten years later, he seized it. The sea became his wife and mistress because he could count on the sea. The sea would never betray him as his brother and wife once had.

All of that had changed when he saw Ibo and the prince near a spring of fresh water. Now his affections were being wooed away from the sea and being transferred to flesh and blood—but he didn't know it.

Chapter 26

Francois and Helen Torvell

On August 22, 1791, the Windward docked at the Isle of Santo Domingo and unloaded its cargo. It had been nearly one hundred years since the French officially colonized the island in 1697; more than two hundred years since Christopher Columbus "discovered" it in 1492 and began the Spanish colonization. Of the island's five hundred thousand people, only five percent were wealthy white planters; four percent were free people of color, better known as the *gens de couleur;* ninety percent were slaves—and that was an enormous powder keg. Indigenous insurgents called the Maroons had been successfully practicing guerilla warfare on the planters for years. For more than two hundred years whites ruled and prospered, but tonight, things would change forever—the insurgency would see to it.

Captain Rutgers was well aware of the instability of the island, but there was good money to be made. In a million years he would have never thought that a group of so-called ignorant blacks could have taken back the island now called Haiti. He had no idea that that very night, the leader of the Maroons, with the help of house slaves, were planning an unprecedented move that would eventually free the Isle of Santo Domingo of white rule. Had he known that, had he any inkling that white planters, their families, and whites in general were going to be savagely murdered, he would not have agreed to sell the prince to his friend and Christian brother, Monsieur Francois Torvell.

Of the six hundred slaves the ship could carry, only four hundred made it to the Isle of Santo Domingo alive. The number was expected. It was a difficult voyage for the slaves, and many died or jumped into the sea on the way.

The slaves had been cramped in the cargo hold for the better part of three months and had to be cleaned of the filth and stench that clung to them. They cleaned the slaves by throwing buckets of water on them, which helped, but was far from doing the job necessary. The way they smelled skewed the way the planters saw them. They smelled like animals, so that's what they became in the eyes of their masters. At the very least they were seen as savages; anything but the human beings they were.

When they thought the slaves were sufficiently cleansed and presentable, they marched them to Monsieur Torvell's plantation. Captain Rutgers rode in a carriage. Ibo rode with him, right by his side. He wanted to show her off to his friend, who, he knew, would be quite envious. Torvell didn't have to know there was no sex going on between them. The assumption was good enough for Rutgers. With nearly twenty-two thousand free people of color on the island, it wasn't at all unusual for a black woman to be seen openly with a white man.

Monsieur Torvell was a tobacco man. He was the son of Jacques Torvell, who had come to the Isle of Santo Domingo forty years earlier. Jacques Torvell was a swindler by trade. He brought a sack full of money to the island and bought the land and a few slaves to work it for next to nothing. Now the Torvells owned the biggest tobacco plantation on the island. Business was booming, and they needed another hundred slaves in addition to the three hundred they already had to bring in a much larger crop.

Darkness was nearly upon them by the time they arrived. Rutgers pulled the reins and stopped the carriage in front of a lavish white brick mansion. The grounds were well maintained and pristine. Monsieur Torvell and Helen, his wife of twenty years, greeted them. Behind them stood their black butler, Herman, and his wife, Marcia, whom they trusted with their lives and their financial portfolio. They lived in the mansion and practically ran the plantation. When Torvell wanted to know something about his property, his servants, or anything other than Mrs. Torvell, he went to Herman for answers. Helen considered Marcia a close friend. They often had lunch together. Consequently, they saw nothing wrong with what they were doing, since two of their best friends on the island—in the world, for that matter—were Negroes. Besides, they had given them the Torvell name, and that made them officially family, didn't it?

Chapter 27

"Don't tell me we have royalty with us."

Now, when Helen saw Ibo sitting next to Rutgers, she looked at Francois to see his reaction to her good looks. He was obviously enamored by Ibo's beauty. His lecherous smile confirmed it for her. Helen was hoping that she wasn't a part of the cargo they had just purchased, because her husband was known for his escapades with the dusky females they owned. She didn't want another one on the island that she would have to compete with for her husband's affections. While it wasn't officially acknowledged, she was the reluctant stepmother of more than ten pickaninnies that looked remarkably like Francois.

Feeling quite vulnerable at the moment, she shot a quick glance at her supposed new rival. From what Helen could tell, she was the kind of female who was used to men staring at her. She deduced that Ibo had the kind of looks that made it nearly impossible not to stare at her.

That's what she told herself anyway. As far as she was concerned, she had nothing to worry about. The woman saw her husband as just another man that she knew found her extremely attractive.

With her inner fears aside, she forced a quick smile and hugged their friend who had dismounted. She kissed both of his cheeks and in French, she said, "Joseph, it's so good to see you." Her voice had an air of aristocratic sophistication in it; like someone had paid a fortune for her education.

He embraced her and said, "It's good to see you both as well."

"And who is this beautiful creature?" Helen asked.

Rutgers smile broadly and said, "Ibo Mustafa. She's my personal guest aboard the Windward." He extended his hand to help Ibo down the carriage stairs.

"Your next stop must be New Orleans, Joseph," Francois said, smiling.

Having been there, he knew miscegenation ran rampant there. They even had special balls for the occasion; balls where beautiful, light-skinned black females were taken specifically to be a wealthy white man's exclusive consort. If he were living in New Orleans, he'd do everything he could to be her lover.

"It is, sir," Rutgers said. "And I'm sure she'll fetch a great price."

"Well, you all made it just in time for dinner," Helen said, quickly changing the subject. The last thing she wanted to hear was men sexualizing women in her presence. To do it in private was bad enough, but to do it openly was a shameful thing for good Christians to do. "Marcia made a great dinner for us. I hope you're hungry."

"We are," Rutgers said. "Famished, in fact. I've been looking forward to eating some of Marcia's scrumptious cooking since I was last here."

Helen hooked her arm around Rutgers' elbow and escorted him toward the house. Then she looked at Marcia and said, "Please see to it that Miss Mustafa wants for nothing."

While Ibo was just as hungry as Rutgers was, she hadn't seen the prince in weeks. He still consumed her thoughts and dreams daily. She wanted to see him before they left him there. She wanted him to know that while she would wait for him, she had a plan of her own to rescue him, if need be.

Respectfully, Ibo, in French, said, "Captain Rutgers, if it's okay with you, I'd like to see the prince now."

"She speaks French?" Francois asked rhetorically.

"That and about four or five other languages," Rutgers said. "It's a gift. She's a quick study. She could probably run this plantation better than Herman here inside of a month."

"You don't say," Francois said. "I see why you expect a great deal of compensation for her. Tell me your price and I will pay it."

Rutgers cut his eyes toward Helen briefly and said, "I've already got a buyer in New Orleans. I can't very well go back on my word, can I?"

"Not even for a longtime friend like me?"

"I'm afraid not. It would be unethical. Besides, how could I expect to continue doing business with the man if he found out what I did?"

"Yes, Joseph," Helen said, glaring at Francois. "By all means, stick to your principles."

"A prince, huh?" Francois questioned, changing the subject to appease his jealous wife. "And who might that be?"

"Yes, Joseph," Helen said, smiling broadly. "Don't tell me we have royalty with us."

"In a manner of speaking, I guess we do have royalty with us," Rutgers said. "As a matter of fact, he's a part of the cargo you paid for, Francois."

"Really?" Helen said. She looked at her husband. "Well, I'd like to see this prince. Wouldn't you, dear?"

"Yes, I would," Francois said. "But first, let's have a bite to eat and some of our vintage wine." He looked at Rutgers. "Herman can show your guest to the servants' quarters."

Chapter 28

"It's the natural order of things."

"The man you're looking for...is he really a prince?" Herman asked Ibo in French.

"Yes. The king had many sons, and Amir was one of them."

"So what's your story?" Herman asked as they walked along the path that led to the slave quarters.

"My story?"

"Yes. I've been on this island all my life long, and if there's one thing I know, everybody has a story. So what's yours?"

She told him how she and Amir became the property of Captain Rutgers. She told him of all the things that happened on the ship and how she and the captain became friends. They weren't actually friends, at least not in her eyes, but she would maintain the façade because it was necessary. Allowing Rutgers to think they were friends was useful for now.

She didn't know Herman and she didn't trust him. There was no way she would trust a man who worked gleefully for a man who enslaved him and then called him a servant, as if he were being paid for the jobs he did. For all she knew, he could be trying to get information out of her. It would be a very long time before she would trust anyone other than Amir.

"What's your name, sir?" Ibo asked, even though she'd heard it when Francois told him to show her where the servants' quarters were. It was a calculated attempt to get information out of him. She wanted to know what languages he spoke so that when she spoke to the prince, she would know whether she would have to disguise what she was really saying.

"Herman."

"What's your last name, Herman?"

"Torvell."

"Torvell? The same name as the man I just met."

"Yes."

"No, I mean your real last name. The one you were born with. What was it before it was Torvell?"

"To my knowledge, it has always been Torvell. We were friends when we were little boys. Monsieur Torvell's father owned my father and mother, and his son owns me and my wife. That's the way things are here."

"And your father never told you who you were? Your family name and where your people came from?"

Herman frowned. "I don't think he knew either." He had never even considered the questions before now. As they continued walking, he thought about the questions. Then he said, "I don't know that it makes a difference, ma'am. I'm here now, and that's all that matters. Monsieur Torvell and his wife treat me and my wife almost like family, and that's good enough for me, I guess."

"Well . . . did your father at least teach you your language?"

"The only language I know is the French language, ma'am."

Good. "What about your wife? Was she born here too?"

"Yes. We grew up together. Monsieur Torvell thought we would make a wonderful couple. He put us together and we've been together ever since."

"So did you have to marry her? Did you have a choice?"

"I suppose I could have said no, but Marcia's a good woman. She's been good to me. We're happy together."

Ibo knew then to change the subject. She had gotten the information she wanted without him suspecting anything—a lesson she had picked up from Iago, a character in *Othello.*

She quickly deduced that Herman had no desire for freedom, which made him a potential enemy. What made matters worse was that he actually thought he could be happy in captivity. She would be as pleasant as she could be, in case he was indeed a spy. If he was a spy, she wanted him to tell the Torvells and Rutgers that she was sweet and accommodating. She wanted them to be relaxed, just as Amir had told her months ago. And when they least expected it, they would come out of the shadows and crush them—Herman too.

"How long will you be here, ma'am?"

"A few days, I guess. I'm not really sure. Why?"

"Because the slaves are restless. I think the Maroons might be attacking again soon."

"The Maroons?"

"Yes, ma'am. They're a bunch of savages bent on killing good Christians for no good reason."

"By good Christians, do you mean the Torvells?"

"Yes, me and Marcia too."

"Is that what they told you?"

"No, the field slaves and the house slaves don't get along, ma'am. But I've seen enough to know that we have reason to be watchful."

"You mean none of the slaves get along?"

"No. We don't trust them and they don't trust us. A woman that looks as good as you might as well get used to it. I suspect that you'll be working in the house when you get to New Orleans, ma'am. That would make you a house slave. I don't think it'll be any different there than here. Besides . . . I think the white folk prefer it that way. Makes them feel safe when we don't get along."

"You have no desire to be free, Herman? You have no desire to come and go as you please?"

"Not really. Things are fine just the way they are. It's the natural order of things, Monsieur Torvell says. I love the Torvells and they treat us good, as I said before. We live in the big house. We eat well. We get to wear the Torvells' hand-me-downs. It's a nice life.

"When you get to New Orleans, you'll see what I mean. Good-looking woman like you won't have to work in the field. You'll be your master's bed wench. As long as he's happy with you, you'll have the best that a black woman can get.

"Anyway, I think it best you stay on the ship at night for however long you're here."

Curious, she asked, "Why? You think the Maroons would hurt me? I have done nothing to make them attack me, Herman."

"If you're having dinner in the big house, you're in danger. The Maroons will think you helped the Torvells, and that would be reason enough to kill you."

"Would you help the Torvells?"

"Yes, I most certainly would. As I said, the Maroons are savages. They have to be stopped. They'll kill good people like Monsieur Torvell and his wife. If it came down to it, I would protect the Torvells before I'd protect Marcia."

They finally reached the barn where they kept the newly acquired slaves. They had to be broken before they could be trusted enough to take off their chains. He slid the door to the left and they walked in. The barn was dark, but she could see many figures moving; she heard chains clanging.

"Amir, I'm here," Ibo called out to him in Yoruba, their native tongue. "Where are you, my love? I have wonderful news."

"I am here . . . in the darkness," he said. "Come to me, my love."

She practically ran to his voice.

They embraced and held each other for a while. It felt so good to be together after all they had been through. They wished the moment would go on forever, that reality would fade away and only their world of fantasy would remain.

As she held on to him, it became clear that he had lost

a lot of weight. She was almost glad that it was dark in the barn. She didn't want to see what had become of him. She felt guilty for eating good, healthy food, even though that's what he had told her to do while he languished in the belly of hell.

Amir held her by the shoulders and said, "The man with you . . . is he a friend or an enemy?"

She shook her head and said, "Unfortunately, he is an enemy, he and his wife, but he does not know it."

"Then it's not safe to talk in front of him," Amir said, lowering his voice.

"He was born here. He doesn't understand. Now, listen quickly. We don't have much time. There's a group of men who can help you escape from here. They're called the Maroons. Find out from those who live here how you can join them. I'm sure they can use a man who was the captain of the Dahomey Imperial Army. I will be going to a place called New Orleans. When you free yourself, keep your promise and find me. If I get free first, I will come to this place and find you."

Chapter 29

"You mean the way you thanked me for saving yours?"

Herman, Marcia, and Ibo were in the kitchen eating the delicious apple pie Marcia had prepared for the Torvells when several members of the Maroons kicked in the back door, machetes in hand. Stunned by what had happened so incredibly quickly, Ibo stood up. Her eyes bulged. Her mouth fell open.

Marcia was about to scream when one of the Maroons sliced her vocal cords. Blood pumped out of her neck. Gagging, she grabbed her throat and squeezed. Blood leaked out of the corners of her mouth and slid down her chin. Her eyes rolled back into her head. Then she fell dead onto the floor.

Herman had grabbed the other man and wrestled the machete away from him. Then he plunged it into his stomach. Almost as soon as he stuck the machete in, another man grabbed him from behind and sliced through his throat.

That's when Ibo came to her senses and ran out of the kitchen. She ran right into Captain Rutgers, who had heard the commotion. The man came at Rutgers with the machete, but Rutgers was ready for him. When the man tried to slash his throat, he stepped in and wrapped his arm around the man's arm and back-fisted him. The machete clanged to the floor.

Rutgers tried to grab the machete, but the man stuck out his hand and tripped him. He fell hard to the floor. The man climbed on top of him and pounded his face. But when he went for the machete, somehow Rutgers found the strength to grab his arm when it was only an inch or two away from the bloodied weapon. Each man struggled to break free of the other.

Rutgers arched his back, lifting the man up and to the left, away from the machete. Once the man was off balance, Rutgers was able to flip him over and gain the advantage. He pummeled the man's face until it was a bloodied mess. Then he grabbed the machete and plunged it into his chest.

Rutgers heard Helen screaming in the dining room, which was only a few feet from the kitchen. He heard a musket fire. He ran in there and saw several large Negroes. Two of them were attacking Helen and Ibo, ripping off their clothes. The breasts of both women were exposed. A third man had taken Francois' musket from him and was on top of him, beating him senseless with it. He grabbed the man who was attacking Ibo first and snapped his neck.

One of the Negro men had Helen on the floor. Her

dress was up; her panties torn off. The Negro was inside her already, plowing vigorously. Rutgers was about to help Helen when several more angry Negro men poured into the house. He grabbed Ibo by the hand and they ran for their lives. Outside now, they saw a lot more Negroes running toward them.

Quickly, he picked up Ibo and put her in the carriage. Just as he was about to get in, the Negro who had beaten Francois to death grabbed him, and they fell to the ground. He elbowed the man in the nose and the man let go. Then Rutgers stood up. He tried to get into the carriage again, but the man grabbed his foot. Rutgers turned around and kicked the man in the face. He let go and fell backward.

Another Negro ran and tried to dive on him, but Rutgers saw him. He bent his knees at just the right time, grabbed the man while he was in the air, stood up, and tossed the man into several other men running toward him. They all fell backward to the ground.

Rutgers quickly jumped into the carriage, grabbed the reins, and pulled off in haste. As the carriage pulled off, they looked through the window and saw the Negroes who had poured into the house standing in a line, waiting to take their turn with Helen Torvell. Rutgers knew that if those men hadn't stopped to ravage their former mistress, he and Ibo would have been brutally murdered too.

More men were coming. There didn't seem to be an end to them. He ran the horses into some of them and still they came, determined to kill them both.

By the time they made it back to the ship, it looked as

if the entire island was ablaze. Rutgers stopped the carriage at the dock. They got out and quickly headed up the gangplank to the ship.

Breathing heavily, he said, "We're even now. You saved my life and I just saved yours."

Holding her torn dress to cover her naked breasts, Ibo remained silent. She breathed in his fear, swallowing it whole; savoring it like it was the delicious apple pie she'd eaten before the Maroons barged in. The look in his eyes gave her the confidence to pursue the plans she had made to turn the tables on her pasty tormentors.

Nevertheless, she was wise enough to hide the pleasure she was experiencing, knowing that if he thought she was relishing any part of what the Maroons did to the Torvells, he would probably renege on the deal and sell her to a wicked plantation owner.

Angry about what the Maroons did to his friends, he grabbed her by the arm and shouted, "I want to hear you say we're even."

He had never been so scared in his life. He thought he was dead for sure. What frightened him most was the thought of being taken alive by the Maroons. The idea of losing power, losing control to men of color, men whom he was used to beating into submission, made his hair stand up. While he drove the carriage back to the docks, he had imagined being tied to a post of some sort and tortured with a whip, being beaten to within an inch of his life, much like he had done numerous times.

Glad to be alive and sensing the need to show deference, she looked at him and said, "We're even, Captain."

She knew she had to give every indication that Captain

Rutgers was still in control. She knew he needed to be—or at least feel like he was. She would supply that need, because she now knew a truth that had eluded her. The Maroons' rebellion had taught her a valuable lesson. She now knew that the person who relinquished control was the person in control, not the other way around. She now knew that giving up control was always temporal. Control could be seized again at any moment, and more could be taken in the process. She therefore gave him the respect he wanted, and in so doing, controlled her fate in New Orleans without Rutgers ever knowing she was now in charge.

Still angry, he said, "I think a little gratitude is in order."

"Gratitude?"

"Yes. A thank you."

"You mean the way you thanked me for saving yours?"

"Hmpf . . . well . . . as long as you know we're even."

As the ship set sail, Ibo stood on the deck, holding her torn dress over her breasts as she watched the island burn. She wondered what would become of Amir and how many people had died that night. She hoped that the rebellion would be successful for Amir's sake. He was a warrior, so she knew he would survive. That's what she believed anyway. But if the whites ever regained control of the island, they would put all the rebels to death, she knew.

Then she remembered his final words to her in the barn: "Stay alive and I will come for you. No matter how long it takes. I will come for you." She took comfort in his words. She would stay alive. She would hold on to his love and believe that one day they would see each other again.

And if necessary, she would come back to the island to find him.

Still covering her breasts, she walked across the deck of the Windward and down the stairs. Her newly discovered truth made her feel like she was floating on a cloud. She entered Rutgers' quarters, changed clothes, and sat in one of the spoon-back chairs. Then she did her best to remember everything she had seen.

She focused primarily on the rape of Helen Torvell. She had now seen two of them, but the second rape gave her an immense sense of satisfaction. As far as she was concerned, turnabout was fair play. What she didn't know was that with each act of brutality she witnessed, her heart was hardening—and the repercussions of that would reveal themselves in her future.

Part 2

Bouvier Hill

Chapter 30

The Humiliation of Remembrance

And there she was, standing on the auction block, looking into the faces of the men who wanted to permanently purchase her goods and make them their very own, like she was some life-sized, black-faced doll to whom they could do all the nasty things they imagined in their wicked hearts. While they were thinking about her, she was thinking about her precious Amir and whether he was even alive. Full of hope, she trusted that someday they would be together.

In a strange way, not knowing what became of him was worse than knowing. If she knew for certain that he was dead, at least there would be a measure of closure. If she knew for certain that he was dead, she could hold on to the memory of him and yet extricate herself from him at the same time. She could move on emotionally and figure out how she would gain her freedom on her own. But if she knew Amir was still alive and trying to keep his promise to come for her, that bit of information would strengthen her resolve to resist those who would enslave her in any way she could. Knowing he was alive would keep her alive, and give her hope for a future with him.

She looked down at the men and listened as their lively clamor rose in volume. She felt the need to release all the turmoil going on inside her heart. She hadn't seen her family in more than four months. She missed her older sisters, her brothers, and her mother and father. She missed her home and her own little corner in the house on the farm where they lived. What she missed most was the freedom to come and go as she pleased; to so much as relieve herself without having to tell her captor why she needed a few minutes to herself.

Telling Rutgers why she needed a few minutes or longer made it easy to figure out if she needed to urinate or defecate. And that was so *very* personal. Her own father didn't know when she had to relieve herself, yet this Dutchman not only knew when she had to go, but could figure out which of the two she needed to do. It was *so* humiliating.

The beginnings of tears were starting to form, but she fought them off, remembering that she was in control. She refused to give those who would buy her the satisfaction of seeing her at her weakest moment. She refused to let them see how broken she felt, how absolutely alone she felt, even though there were plenty of people in that place who resembled her; people who had her skin tone and facial features. When she felt her heart was at the point of shattering as if it were fine, expensive crystal, she fought off the ocean of tears by remembering how strong

Amir had been when the crew of the Windward tossed their disposable slaves to the powerful jaws of the man-eating sharks that patiently waited for their meal, and she found the strength she needed to journey on.

The highest bid was now at two thousand dollars. Ibo had no idea how much that was. In Dahomey, they didn't use painted paper as currency. They used cowry shells and goods as legal tender. She looked at the man who had bid what many in the burgeoning crowd thought was an outrage. He was standing next to Captain Rutgers, who was saying something to a different man and pointing at her. She naturally assumed that the man was Monsieur Beaumont Bouvier. He was well-dressed, sporting a pair of cream-colored trousers, a cream-colored vest, and navy tails. But he was very short. He was five feet one inch in shoes.

As she listened to her price rise higher and higher, she noticed that the black man in the fancy clothes, the one the people standing around him called Massa, was coming over to the auction market. His name was Walker Tresvant.

Chapter 31

A Vengeful Plot

Walker Tresvant was a multimillionaire; one of several black men in New Orleans to be so distinguished. He had been educated at the Sorbonne in Paris and was the owner of a very large sugarcane plantation.

He had been standing too far away to see how beautiful the woman on the auction block was, and had only gone over because he heard the bidding amounts and they intrigued him. He had to see what all the commotion was about. He had to see what the white men were going to get for all that money they were about to spend on one slave girl.

When he saw her hypnotic, deep-set eyes, her long, slender neck, and the thick cushions disguised as lips, he had joined the bidding; however, when the amount reached seventeen hundred dollars, he withdrew and watched to see which of his competitors would acquire her "services." He had never seen any slave go for more than seventeen hundred dollars. To his recollection, he had only seen one slave even approach that number, and he was a man—a prime black buck of a man, a studding buck of a man, one that could keep the women on the plantation barefoot and pregnant.

While he could understand why the men wanted to bed her and were willing to pay handsomely to do so, he didn't understand why they allowed their sexual proclivities to get in the way of a sound business decision. The woman on the block could only have one or two children at a time, at the most three, and then she couldn't have more until nearly a year later. A stud could get one woman with child, and then keep producing children as long as there were women to impregnate.

If a planter was fortunate enough to have ten, perhaps twenty women pregnant months or weeks apart, a prime studding buck could start the pregnancy cycle over and over again. At that rate, he could get somewhere between twenty and forty slaves to work the plantation for the cost of one buck. Paying nearly seventeen hundred dollars for one like that made all the business sense in the world. It was a good investment. The woman on the block, while she possessed incredible beauty, couldn't be seen as an investment on future children the way a stud could.

"The bid is two thousand," the auctioneer said. "Do I hear two thousand one hundred?" There was considerable grumbling, but no one bid. "Two thousand once . . . two thousand twice . . ."

"Twenty-five hundred," Beaumont said, and raised his white handkerchief.

Monsieur Bouvier was a third generation Frenchman

from Monaco. One hundred years earlier, Damien Bouvier, his grandfather, who had been a renowned baker,
wanted more for himself and his family and made plans to
stake his claim on some of the vast real estate he had
heard about.

When he had saved enough money for the voyage, he
set sail for the New World, with grandiose dreams of becoming a success in a place called North America. He
opened a bakery, and business boomed. He soon learned,
however, that slavery was far more profitable and one
could live like a member of the House of Grimaldi of
Monaco.

When Tresvant saw Beaumont bid, he raised his hand,
indicating that he was bidding twenty-six hundred. He
wasn't going to buy the woman. He just wanted to make
Beaumont pay considerably more because the Bouviers
had once owned his family.

Tresvant's grandfather was the first slave that Damien
Bouvier purchased—that's the story that had been
handed down to the third generation. His name was
Alexander Tresvant Bouvier, and he served Damien faithfully for two years.

One day, Alexander saw a lovely octoroon on a neighboring plantation. Her name was Jennifer. He made in-
quires and learned that she was a nineteen-year-old
maiden with no man in her life other than her father.
After Alexander got permission to court her, they fell
completely in love over the course of three wonderful
months. Alexander asked her father for her hand in marriage, and he was agreeable. He then asked Master Bou-

vier to purchase her so he could marry her and start a family.

Bouvier agreed immediately. But on the night of their honeymoon, Bouvier told the young man that he would have to bed her first, and then Alexander could have her afterward. When Bouvier saw the astonished look on Alexander's face, he explained that he had an insatiable penchant for virgins.

Gleefully, he told Alexander, "There's nothing like being the first to break a virgin in. That's something you could never fully appreciate. Besides, I paid two hundred dollars for her. It's only fair I get a crack at her first." It never even occurred to Bouvier that Alexander wanted to be the first and only man his wife knew intimately.

The salacious visual ran through the young man's mind in an instant and crushed his spirit. Being a slave afforded him no formal rights as a husband, and therefore, he was powerless to keep them both from being violated. They didn't know it at the time, but they would wear visible emotional scars as if they were clothing—and so would their children.

On their wedding night, when the time came to step aside and allow his master to enter his wife, Alexander refused her and avoided the act. He didn't have the heart to tell Jennifer what was going to happen to her—to them.

Jennifer had been looking forward to joining with him and was confused. She wondered why he was taking so long to consummate the marriage. When Bouvier enter their house without knocking, knowing they were on their honeymoon, Jennifer looked at her husband, expecting him to do or at least say something. But he didn't. He just bowed his head and left immediately without a word of explanation. Her eyes nearly bulged out of her head when she realized what was about to happen.

"No, Massa," she said when he started taking off his clothes.

Bouvier acted as if he didn't hear her and continued undressing. Twenty minutes or so later, he left their house and made his way back to his own bed, where his wife, who knew what was going on, waited in silence.

While Tresvant's grandparents stayed together, their relationship was never the same because not only did Bouvier take his grandfather's right as a husband, but he didn't keep his word. After that initial encounter with Jennifer, he continued seeing her regularly for well over a year. Sometimes he'd stay the entire night.

Jennifer's attitude changed, and Alexander wanted to know why. One night, he stood outside an open window and listened to them grunt and groan. Much of the music he heard came from Jennifer, who was obviously enraptured by what they were doing *together.* When Alexander realized that his wife had somehow learned to enjoy the impromptu visits, he was enraged and decided he would have his revenge.

Chapter 32

"Do enjoy her, if you can."

Alexander Bouvier pretended to be the best servant his master ever had, knowing full well he was going to return the favor someday, even if the debt would be repaid by his own son or daughter vicariously. He asked for and had been granted special permission to hire himself out on weekends, doing whatever laborious work he could find to earn enough money to buy himself and his wife. He worked seven days a week. Sometimes, when work was available, he hired out his evenings during the week in an effort to expedite his family's freedom.

It took five years to accomplish this because he had to give half his earnings to Bouvier. By then, they had three children. One of them, a lovely blond, blue-eyed girl, obviously belonged to their master. Before they realized the baby was sired by Damien Bouvier, they had decided to name her Julia. But when Bouvier learned that the baby was his, he loved her, and named her Kayla, after his grandmother.

When Alexander had saved enough money to pay for his wife and children, including Kayla, Bouvier gave him two teams of horses, two wagons, which he strung together, and all the supplies Alexander could carry to start a new life. Altruism had little if anything to do with his magnanimity. The gifts were a way to assuage a mind saturated with guilt. They were born of a mind that had come to terms with what he had done to a man who had served him faithfully for many years.

As a final gift, Bouvier gave back all the money Alexander had been paying him over the years for their freedom. He told him he had saved it for him as a surprise and for his own good, just in case something happened to his savings.

Later, after they left New Orleans, Alexander dropped the name Bouvier and became known as Alexander Tresvant. He moved his family west to the Rocky Mountains of what later became the Colorado Territory, where he met a different group of Christians who not only believed what the Bible said, but actually practiced its commandments. They sold him land, educated him and his family, and taught them that all men were of one blood. Over the course of time, he found gold on his property, long before The Pike's Peak Gold Rush in 1861, which later became known as the Colorado Gold Rush.

Alexander then hired several white Christian attorneys he trusted to procure vast amounts of land in New Orleans, where he later produced sugar and became a wealthy plantation owner. By the time he and his family moved back to New Orleans, Damien Bouvier had died. As far as Alexander was concerned, when Damien bequeathed his land and money to his progeny, he also left them his debt and dishonor. He had read that legally, when a person is left anything in a will, the person takes responsibility for debt as well as assets. And so revenge would be taken on those he left behind when he went to his grave.

Beaumont heard the bid and looked to see who dared offer more than he. When he saw Walker Tresvant's bright white teeth against his rich mahogany skin, he glared at him and then raised his handkerchief again, offering a bid of twenty-seven hundred. He didn't like Walker because he threatened to bring shame on the Bouvier name by seducing his sister, Marie-Elise, and impregnating her. Then Walker made sure that it was the talk of the parish, so that if she did not marry him, which was fine with him, everyone would know her condition and who had gotten her in it if the baby somehow disappeared after it was born.

Beaumont's dislike of Walker wasn't a color issue. In eighteenth century New Orleans, money trumped race. If Walker had loved her, Beaumont would have been okay with the marriage.

The ensuing scandal was legendary, as Marie-Elise was engaged at the time to Mason Beauregard. The Beauregards were one of New Orleans' leading families. Their joining was supposed to be one that would solidify their enormous wealth and make it possible to expand by buying out as many small plantations as they could. Walker knew this, and pounced on her as if she were a delectable slice of sweet honeydew melon. He found her to be easy pickings because she did not love Mason, nor did she want to marry him. The marriage was sham. It was being foisted on her as her duty as a Bouvier, nothing more.

Marie-Elise Bouvier's pregnancy was the sweetest revenge, as this was what Damien had done to Jennifer two generations earlier. It also served as a permanent divider of two of the wealthiest families in New Orleans, making it possible for Walker Tresvant to buy the smaller plantations while the Beauregards and the Bouviers were at each other's throats. He loved it, laughing uncontrollably whenever he thought of it. Were it not for the Tresvants' considerable wealth, Walker would have been castrated and lynched—in that order.

Instead, the whole episode was legitimized by a gala spectacle of a wedding to save the face of the Bouvier clan. The Bouvier money was able to secure the presence of several mayors, judges, and politicians from as far away as New York City and Chicago, in addition to every influential family in New Orleans—except the Beauregards. This was by no means the first interracial marriage of a black man and a white woman in New Orleans. It was, however, the first one where an affluent white woman from a powerful family married the offspring of a slave that the aforementioned family formerly owned.

The wedding was the social event of the summer and practically shut down the city as if it were a holiday. If the Bouviers wanted a business owner at the wedding and he didn't close his store that day, they threatened to run him out of business—all of this to hide the shameful truth that

Marie-Elise was already pregnant with Walker Tresvant's child and couldn't marry Mason Beauregard.

Marie-Elise did not have to marry Walker, but if she didn't, she would have suffered public humiliation for being with child without the benefit of marriage. Later, when she had the baby, everyone would know the father was a nigger, which would have been more humiliating. Marrying a rich nigger and then having his baby solved everything. Besides, she adored Walker and was happy to have him as a husband.

Part of the reason she had premarital sex with him was because she hated being sold into a form of slavery by her own father. Allowing Walker to bed her, and in due course impregnate her, liberated her, and demoralized those who sought to gain from her misery.

Still gazing at Walker, Beaumont thought he was trying to buy himself a beautiful bed wench to humiliate his younger sister. To prevent that from happening, he believed he had to continue bidding no matter what price he had to pay. Walker knew this and continued bidding to aggravate his brother-in-law. The two men continued bidding back and forth until her price reached five thousand dollars; twice as much as what Beaumont would have paid had Walker not gotten involved.

"Congratulations, dear brother," Walker said, smiling broadly. "Do enjoy her, if you can." Then he laughed uproariously.

Chapter 33

Farewell, Captain Rutgers

"You're going to be all right," Rutgers said to Ibo.

"Am I, Captain?" she said, staring unflinchingly in his eyes.

"I'm a man of my word," Rutgers said. "He paid an enormous sum for you and promised me he would treat you well."

"So long as I cooperate, right, Captain?" she said, firing lightning bolts with her eyes.

"I don't think you'll have to worry about that," Rutgers said, smiling.

"Oh, really? And here I was thinking that that was why you kept me unspotted," she said. "Just when I thought being unblemished brought you a greater price, you were actually worried about me."

"It did. As I said, he paid a lot of money for you . . . nearly ten times your worth. You can thank the feud between Tresvant and the man who bought you for the drastic price increase."

"Feud? Between a black man and a white man? Hmmm. Then it is as you have said here. Free blacks with money are treated almost like whites."

"In Walker Tresvant's case, exactly the same. I've done good by you. You'll see that later."

Having paid the auctioneer the agreed upon price, Beaumont Bouvier walked over to where his friend and his property stood. He raised his handkerchief, signaling the driver of his horse drawn carriage.

"I guess this is goodbye," Rutgers said and took her hand in his, kissing it gently.

"Good-bye, Captain," she said.

The carriage stopped about fifteen feet from where they were standing. Beaumont told his driver to put her trunk on the carriage. Then he politely escorted his newly purchased bed wench to his carriage. He helped her climb in and then got into it himself.

Rutgers looked at her one last time and said, "Remember our discussions and you'll be just fine." He was referring to Shakespeare's plays and the lessons she learned from them. They were supposed to help her gain her freedom in the years to come. "Do you understand?"

"I have always understood you, Captain," she said without looking at him. "I am not sure if you ever understood me."

"Farewell, my friend," Rutgers said to Beaumont.

"May you experience calm seas on your journeys," Beaumont said.

Rutgers tapped the carriage twice, signaling to the driver that it was okay to pull off. He stood there in the auction market and watched the carriage until it disappeared. Then he went back to the auction block and watched the bidding for his other slaves, carefully keeping records of what each slave sold for. While he stood there watching and listening, from time to time he thought about Ibo Atikah Mustafa and hoped that she would one day be free.

Chapter 34

"Lauren Renee Bouvier."

Beaumont Bouvier was a very meticulous man, believing wholeheartedly in ancient Greek philosophy, especially the works of Socrates, his student, Plato, and his student, Aristotle, who taught Alexander the Great. Aristotle's ideas on virtue and the greater good, along with Greek slavery, shaped his thinking; it was how he justified his part in the practice of American slavery. He believed that if the enlightened Greek society was in large part a society that functioned mainly by the labor of slaves, there couldn't be anything wrong or evil about it.

Being a student of history, politics, and philosophy, he treated his slaves the same way the Greeks treated theirs, which was why he seldom used the whip as an instrument of discipline, preferring rather to sell the difficult slave to a master who had no compunction. He believed in order, discipline, and fair play. As long as his slaves did their jobs, were obedient, and brought no shame on the Bouvier name, they were treated well. Some were even allowed to work in New Orleans on the weekends to earn money to buy their freedom.

On the way home, he stopped by his attorney's office to handle the formal legalities of purchasing chattel, and other formalities concerning the execution of his will, all of which took about an hour and a half. Then he headed out to his sprawling sugarcane plantation, Bouvier Hill.

They entered the gates of Bouvier Hill and made their way up the long path to the immaculate white mansion called Bouvier Manor. The slaves referred to it as the big house. It resembled the residence at 1600 Pennsylvania Avenue, which would begin construction a year from now under President George Washington's administration in October, 1792, and concluded eight years later when John Adams and his wife Abigail moved in.

The plantation grounds were spectacular and nearly perfect in appearance. In the midst of the trees were stables, slave quarters, and sugarcane as far as the eye could see. Between the stables and the slave quarters was the sugar-house. Smoke could be seen billowing from its chimneys. About thirty yards from the mansion were other buildings that made the property look like a small community. In many ways, it was.

Bouvier Hill had more than two hundred slaves; twenty-five of them were skilled carpenters, shoemakers, coopers, blacksmiths, weavers, curriers, sawyers, knitters, stable-hands, and distillers. Additionally, the domestic servants included cooks, maids, launderers, butlers, and personal attendants.

The driver stopped the carriage in front of the mansion. Then he jumped down and opened the door for Monsieur Bouvier. Several slaves, all of them men dressed in fine clothing, waited at attention for him to disembark from the carriage. Bouvier stepped out first and then offered his hand to help Ibo out. When the slaves saw her, they all recoiled a little, looking at each other for answers that none of them had. Then they looked at Bouvier and waited for instructions on what they were to do.

"Aubrey," Beaumont said to his butler.

"Yes, Monsieur Bouvier," Aubrey began. "What is your pleasure, sir?"

"Take . . ." He paused and looked at the young woman he had purchased. "Forgive me, dear. In my haste to get away from Walker Tresvant, I neglected to ask you and Rutgers your name. What are you called?"

"Ibo."

"Ibo?" Beaumont questioned with a disdainful frown. "Oh, dear . . . that will never do. We must come up with a new name for you right away. We so want you to fit in here."

"My name is Ibo Atikah Mustafa."

"Yes, yes. I certainly understand your reluctance to part with it, but you are in America now, and you shall have a name that will help you blend in."

"My name is Ibo Atikah Mustafa," she said defiantly.

Beaumont smiled and said, "I want you to fit in, so I'll let you decide what you want to be called, so long as it is a French name, yes?" She just looked at him unwaveringly. He continued, saying, "How about one of these: Desiree, Simone, Noelle, Gabrielle, Josephine, Jacqueline, Madeline, Danielle, Renee, Celine, Catherine, or perhaps Lauren? You decide, dear. There are so many to choose from, yes?"

Ibo composed herself and remembered that she had to play along until she could gain his confidence and then somehow escape. Even though Rutgers had told her she would be given a new name, she couldn't bring herself to agree to a name change so soon. Agreeing to a name change essentially amounted to a change in identity as far as she was concerned. However, if she didn't agree, she was inviting a lashing like those she had seen aboard the Windward and at the auction market. The last thing she wanted was to have her back butchered by some sadistic slave who enjoyed his work.

She nodded once and said, "I will choose one."

"If you have any trouble remembering any of the names, let me know and I'll help you decide, yes? I don't suspect you will if half of what my friend Joseph says about you is true. He says you speak five languages in addition to dozens of African gibberish. Is that right?"

She nodded. "Yoruba, English, Spanish, French, Portuguese, and Dutch."

"Yes, yes, well, I don't think you'll need the Yoruba around here." Beaumont smiled and looked at Aubrey. "Escort her to my chambers and get her something to eat."

Aubrey frowned and looked at the other well-dressed slaves. Then he bowed slightly and said, "Yes, Monsieur Bouvier." He gestured in the direction of the house with his right hand while still bowed.

"And Aubrey . . ."

"Yes, Monsieur Bouvier?"

His eyes blazed when he said, "See to it that she is extended every courtesy. Every courtesy. Do you understand?"

Aubrey looked at Ibo and said, "Right this way, Mademoiselle Mustafa."

As they walked into the mansion and up the winding staircase, he said, "If you like, I would be happy to help you decide on what you are to be called."

Ibo decided that now would be a good time to pretend to be friendly with the house slaves and gather as much information as she could, so she would be ready when it came time to try to escape to a better place.

She looked at him and said, "Aubrey is it?"

"Yes."

She showed him her beautiful smile to put him at ease before saying, "Of the names that he chose, which one do you like?"

Aubrey returned her smile and then said, "Well, of the names he said, I like Lauren Renee Bouvier. It has a ring to it, don't you think?"

"Lauren Renee Bouvier," she repeated. "Hmmm. It doesn't sound as good as Ibo Atikah Mustafa, but I could learn to like it. Lauren Renee Bouvier. Yes, yes. I think that works well for me, Aubrey. Thank you."

"You're welcome, mademoiselle." He stopped in front of Beaumont's bedroom. As he opened the door, he said, "Now, can I bring you something to eat? You must be quite hungry by now. When did you last eat?"

"Yes, I haven't eaten since yesterday. Please bring me something," she said.

"What would you like?"

"You choose for me. Bring something you would like to eat . . . your favorite meal."

"Sure thing, Lauren," he said, trying out her new name on her.

She smiled.

Then he opened the door for her. She stepped in and saw a naked black man in the bed. He was aroused.

Chapter 35

"Find one that pleases you and get in it . . . now!"

Surprised to see a woman, he covered himself with a white sheet and said, "Where is Monsieur Bouvier, Aubrey?" The eighteen-year-old looked as effeminate as he sounded: soft soprano voice, slender physique, high cheekbones, clean-shaven.

Aubrey said, "Monsieur Bouvier will be here shortly, Louis. He told me to bring her here."

Louis laughed loud and hard before saying, "He told you to bring her here? Here? You can *not* be serious. For what reason, Aubrey?"

He examined her, looking at her from head to toe, trying to think of a cutting remark to wound her. "Well . . . she certainly is pretty, isn't she? But who, pray tell, is this strumpet?"

Aubrey narrowed his eyes. He spoke with much erudition and sophistication when he said, "Why, oh why must you be so rude, Louis? There's no reason for it, seeing that she arrived only minutes ago. Her name is Lauren Renee Bouvier, if you must know—not that it's any of *your* business. And his reasons are his own, dear boy. Now . . . I think you should leave. Run along."

Louis laughed again. "And go *where*?"

Exasperated, Aubrey said, "It's a big house and it has many rooms. Find one that pleases you and get in it . . . now!"

Louis rolled his eyes. "Hmpf. I'll find another room when I hear it from Beaumont himself. Not a second before."

Lauren stood there quietly trying to figure out what was going on. She had no idea that Louis was Monsieur Bouvier's lover. In fact, all the housemen were, including Aubrey. They were to come to him at his beck and call, day or night, and fulfill whatever delicious acts he wished on a moment's notice.

"Louis." Beaumont's voice called out from the hallway, attempting to hide his displeasure with him. "Come out here, please."

Louis frowned, as he was stunned when he learned that Beaumont was in the hallway listening. He smiled victoriously and sang, "Coming." He stood up with a sheet wrapped around him, and walked up to Lauren with his nose in the air. Then he walked around her, sniffing her hind parts.

They were about the same height, nearly six feet tall. He stood almost nose to nose with her, staring unflinchingly into her deep-set eyes. He curled his lips, and then he bent down and sniffed her vagina. He stood erect again, took two steps back, and looked her in the eyes again.

Smiling girlishly, he said, "Oh, no. That . . ."—He pointed below her waist—"will never do." Then he laughed heartily and walked toward the door. He looked over his shoulder to see how much damage he had done and then walked out of the room, leaving the door open so Aubrey and Lauren could hear Beaumont back him up.

"Close the door," Beaumont said tactfully, showing no anger.

Louis closed the door.

Seconds after the door was shut, they could hear them talking, angrily going back and forth, but they couldn't make out what they were saying. Without warning, a thunderous slap echoed in the massive hallway and could be heard in the bedroom, where Aubrey and Lauren were waiting patiently and listening attentively. After the loud slap, they heard Louis give off a high-pitched scream, like a woman being beaten by her husband. Both of them laughed raucously, covering their mouths. Then they heard bare feet running down the hall.

The door opened and Beaumont entered the bedroom. With sincere concern, Beaumont said, "I think I hurt Louis' feelings, Aubrey. Could you check on him and make sure he's okay? He's such a Molly sometimes. I swear."

Then Lauren understood that Beaumont was a homosexual. She remembered what Captain Rutgers had said before they left the slave auction. He had told her she would be all right with Beaumont. She smiled broadly, knowing she wouldn't be raped. It was going to be easier than she thought, being the only woman in the house and not having to have sex with the man who owned the rights to her body.

"Right away, Monsieur Bouvier," Aubrey said and left them alone.

Beaumont looked at his newly acquired beauty and said, "So, have you decided on a name yet?"

She nodded sweetly and said, "Yes, I have."

"Splendid," he said with unrestrained excitement. "What shall we call you?"

"I like Lauren Renee. Aubrey helped me pick it out. He says it has a ring to it. What do you think, Monsieur Bouvier?"

"What a truly excellent choice, my dear girl. Excellent indeed. That is what you shall be called from this day forward. Now . . . Lauren . . . would you be so kind as to remove your clothing?"

Chapter 36

"I will not allow you to defile and pollute me."

Lauren took a couple steps backward and said, "Remove my clothing? I most certainly will not remove my clothing. Not for you I won't."

With little to no emotion he said, "Yes. If I am to deflower you, it would be better if you were nude." He took a few steps forward and added to his cavalier request. "Now . . . would you like me to help you undress?"

"But I thought you liked men. That's why Louis was here, yes?"

"Yes, but I have invested considerable capital in you; mostly to keep you from my brother-in-law. I don't see anything wrong with at least sampling you before anyone else. Who knows?" He was laughing now. "I might get to like it again and have a few pickaninnies with you."

Lauren frowned. She couldn't believe this was happening. Just when she thought she had gotten a respite from lewd men, he was going to rape her, even though he preferred men. He was such a small man, thin, and couldn't have weighed more than a hundred and fifty pounds; she did not fear him, as she was so much taller. As a matter of fact, she thought she could not only defend herself, but that she could whip him if necessary.

She looked in his eyes and said, "No, Monsieur Bouvier. I will not take my clothes off. I will not allow you to defile and pollute me."

Laughing, Beaumont said, "*No?* Dear girl, don't you know that I am your master now? You cannot refuse me. It is your duty to please me in any way I choose. You have no say in the matter. Come now, let me help you undress."

He reached out to touch her, and she snatched away.

"Mmmm. This is going to be so much fun."

"No."

"I see. You're going to make this difficult. Fine. Have it your way."

He turned around and went to the door and locked it. Then he turned back to Lauren. He smiled and said, "We can do this the easy way, or we can do this the hard way. It's up to you."

Determined to subdue her, he fast-walked over to where she was standing and reached out to unbutton her blouse. She slapped his hand.

"Oooh," he said, rubbing his stinging fingers. "It hurts so good."

Her resistance turned him on. He reached out again. And again she slapped his hand. Now he was fully aroused, and she could see that he was.

He went at her again, grabbing her, ripping the sleeve of her dress, one that Amir's mother had made especially for her. When she slapped his face, he stopped suddenly, not expecting it. He rubbed his reddening face and went after her again. This time, she backhanded him on the other side of his face. He was stunned again, but undeterred. He went at her again, grabbing her and throwing her on the bed. They wrestled wildly, each of them trying to get the advantage over the other.

"By God, you are my property, girl!" Beaumont grunted as they struggled on the bed. "And I shall have you!"

"I said no and I mean no," Lauren said as they rolled off the bed and onto the floor.

On top of him now, she slapped his face repeatedly, saying, "Don't make me do this, Monsieur Bouvier. I'll do whatever you say, but not this."

She stopped hitting him and pleaded, "Now, I will let you up if you promise not to touch me in that manner."

In a subdued voice, Beaumont said, "I promise."

She let him up, and he came at her again. Both of them were sweating and grunting again, using whatever means available to conquer each other.

Lauren managed to get Beaumont in a headlock. She held his head in place while she punched him over and over again in his face.

Bing! Bing! Bing! Bing! Bing! Bing!

"You just don't learn, do you?" *Bing! Bing!* "I said no, and that's what I mean." *Bing! Bing! Bing!* "Now . . . if I let you go, will you stop?"

Breathing heavily and smarting from the repeated blows, he said, "Yes."

"You promise?"

"Yes, I promise. Now let me go, girl!"

"That's what you said last time." *Bing! Bing! Bing!* "I'll just make sure." *Bing! Bing! Bing! Bing! Bing!* "Now . . . when I let you go, you're going to stop this, right?"

"Right!"

"Do you swear?"

"I swear. Now let me go!"

She let him go and he came at her again. This time, she balled up her fist and pounded him on the crown of his head as he came at her. His eyes crossed and he fell to the floor. He was out cold.

There was a knock at the door. "Is everything all right in there?" Aubrey asked.

Breathing heavily, Lauren said, "Yes. Everything is all right."

"I have your meal. Shall I bring it in?"

"No. Just leave it out there and I'll get it later. I'm not decent."

There was a long pause.

"Is everything all right, Monsieur Bouvier?"

"Uh, he's sleeping right now, Aubrey. Can you come back later?"

"Sleeping?" He pounded on the door. "Monsieur Bouvier, are you all right?"

"Aubrey, he's asleep. He asked not to be disturbed."

He pounded on the door again. "Open the door this instant. Do you hear me?"

Beaumont opened his eyes and realized that he had been knocked out by a woman. He was thoroughly embarrassed. When he gained his focus, he said, "Aubrey, go away! And do not return until I call for you!"

"Yes, Monsieur Bouvier. I just wanted to make sure you were all right! The girl's dinner—"

"Go *away*, Aubrey!"

They heard heels clicking away from the door.

Beaumont looked at Lauren and smiled. He stood up and looked at her like he was ready to try again.

She said, "Come on, then. I'm ready for you. We can do this all night, but I said no, and that's what I mean. When I get finished whipping you again, I promise I'll do whatever you say. But if we have to fight all night, I'm ready."

He said, "Oh, all right. I just wanted to give it a try. But you better not tell anyone about this, or I'll sell you to a planter who won't be nearly as gracious as I. He'll take a whip to you and carve up your back. And I promise you, you will not look as pretty as you do now. Do you understand?"

She nodded.

"Okay, then." Still looking at her, he shouted, "Aubrey!"

Silence.

"Aubrey!" he shouted again. "I know you're there. You cannot help yourself. It's who you are, dear boy. Answer me!"

"Yes, Monsieur Bouvier."

Beaumont, still looking at Lauren, said, "Do you mind opening the door?"

"How do I know you're not going to try something if I turn my back on you?"

Laughing, he said, "You've got a point. Walk backwards if you must, but do open it for Aubrey."

Lauren kept her eyes on Beaumont as she cautiously walked over to the door. She unlocked and opened it. Aubrey came in.

"I understand that you helped Lauren here choose her name."

With deference, Aubrey said, "Yes, sir. Shall I help her choose another? One that you think would better suit her?"

"No. We both like the name. I want you to show her around the house and the grounds. Give her a tour and let her decide what kind of work she wants to do for us."

"Yes, sir." He looked at Lauren. "Right this way."

Still looking over her shoulder, watching Beaumont to make sure he didn't come after her on the way out, she walked through the open door and into the hallway.

"Oh, and Aubrey," Beaumont said.

"Yes, sir."

"Tell Louis I need him now."

"Right away, Monsieur Bouvier."

"And tell him not to bother dressing. I'll take him as he was when I last saw him."

Chapter 37

"You frail little tart!"

"Since we're already in the house, I'll show you where everything is. Then later, I'll show you the grounds and we'll meet a few people along the way," Aubrey said, smiling as they walked down the hall. "Unless, of course, you prefer to start outside. It's up to you."

Lauren forced herself to smile. She saw being shown the house and the grounds by Aubrey—who, she had already decided, was a sycophant—as a way to get close to him. She sensed he was just like Louis and Beaumont; otherwise, he would have a certain look in his eyes when he looked at her. He didn't have it. So far in her young life, no heterosexual man could deny himself the pleasure of at least gazing at her when they thought she was unaware. The men on Bouvier Hill didn't look at her at all, let alone wantonly.

She wrapped her left arm around his, looked into his

eyes, offered him her disarming smile, and sweetly said, "You decide, Aubrey."

Aubrey was about six three, slender, tight, and midnight black. He was forty-five, extremely well groomed, sporting a thick black moustache. His hair was short and neat.

"Okay, I'll show you the house first and then we'll go outside," he said, returning her smile.

They stopped at a door. He knocked and then opened it. Louis was sitting in a chair on the terrace, still nude, touching himself. He was looking out at Joshua, the blacksmith, who was just outside the stables where Monsieur Bouvier kept his prized stallions. He was shaping a horseshoe. His finely tuned chest and arm muscles flexed each time he struck the iron he held. Louis wanted Joshua, and would do just about anything to have him.

There would be no romantic entanglements between the men, as Joshua was a lover of women: pretty women, voluptuous women, skinny women, ugly women. Joshua enjoyed any woman with whom Monsieur Bouvier paired him. He hated the housemen because they were Bouvier spies and because they were what he called Romans, due to their male on male sexual proclivities. And so Louis just watched him from afar and fantasized day and night of being ravaged powerfully by the blacksmith who ignored his unsolicited advances.

"He wants you now," Aubrey said, interrupting Louis' daily delight.

He stopped his motion, stood up, and turned around. Seeing Lauren in the hallway prompted no modesty. Instead, he pranced around like a runway model, showing off his tall, thin but muscular physique and his engorged tool. He was quite proud of his sexual prowess and how short his refractory time was, making it possible to give and receive well into the night and early again the next day, if need be.

"Where is he?" he asked, smiling triumphantly while looking at Lauren, but talking to Aubrey. He wanted her to know that Beaumont was his, and that he was Beaumont's whenever he wanted, and that no bed wench, no matter how pretty or well-endowed she was, could ever take his place.

"Right where you left him," Aubrey said with venom.

With his hands on his hips, thumbs first, he walked up to Lauren and stood close enough for his tool to touch her stomach without him handling it. He looked down at her and then took another step, pushing her a few steps backward with it.

Locking eyes with her, he said, "I *left* him in the hall-way, Aubrey." He stole a quick peek to the right, and see-ing no one, fastened his eyes on Lauren again and continued. "I don't see him out here. Do you, Aubrey?"

Aubrey pushed his head hard, and Louis stumbled away from Lauren. "You frail little tart! You *know* where he is. Get in there!"

Louis stuck his tongue out at Aubrey and then he turned around and skipped down the hall like a child of six years. When he reached Beaumont's bedroom, he looked back at them to see if they were still watching him. They were. He turned his body to them and mimicked grabbing and pumping the air. Then he laughed a high-pitched, wildly wicked laugh as he entered the room.

Chapter 38

"Just remember, nobody's perfect . . . including you."

Aubrey shook his head like he wished Louis didn't exist, so he couldn't embarrass him or anyone of their ilk. With rancor, he said, "Don't mind him none, Lauren. He doesn't know any better. People like *him* give homosexuality a bad name. People like *him* make it difficult for us all. We have to *hide* who we are because of floozies like him. No man should have to hide who he is. We should be able to be who we are without fear of those who don't understand our tastes."

What these people are doing is an abomination before Almighty God! But I'm going to keep my mouth shut. I'm going to keep my opinion of homosexuality to myself. After all, I might need Aubrey later. He could prove to be a powerful ally. For now, though, I'll pretend to be his friend. I dare not trust the house servants. Herman taught me that much on the Isle of Santo Domingo!

Aubrey gently took her arm and placed it around his

and started walking down the stairs. "So, what kind of work do you like to do, Lauren? What kind of skills do you have?"

"I am a coiffure and couturier," she said confidently.

"Hmm, you don't say. A hairdresser and a dressmaker, huh?"

"In that order, yes, sir."

He raised a brow and said, "Are you any good?"

"Very good, Aubrey," she said and laid her head on his shoulder. "I started watching my mother make clothing when I was about two years old. She recognized that I wanted to do what she was doing, so she started teaching me how when I was five."

"I see, and how old are you now?"

"Almost seventeen," she said like a teenager who wanted to be seen as an adult.

"I see. So you've got ten years experience."

"Almost eleven. But yes, about ten years."

"That's impressive. What about designing? Do you know how to do that, or are you just the type that makes what others create?"

"I make my own clothing."

He looked at her. "Did you make that dress you have on?"

"No. Amir's mother made this for me."

"Who's Amir, and how did the sleeve get torn?"

"Amir is the man I love. We were taken together. He's still on the Isle of Santo Domingo." She forced another smile. "How the sleeve got torn is something you don't need to know about. Right, Aubrey?"

"I guess not."

He showed her most of the house, where everything was, and introduced her to the staff—all of them men.

They were approaching the east wing of Bouvier Manor where the library was. Aubrey said, "You know, I was thinking. You and Mrs. Bouvier could get along great."

"Why do you say that?" She thought for a second and then frowning, she said, "Mrs. Bouvier?"

Aubrey laughed. "You heard me right. Mrs. Bouvier."

Lauren's frown tightened and then loosened when she thought she understood the conundrum. "Oh, okay. He told me he had a sister."

Aubrey laughed again. "He does have a sister, but her name is Mrs. Tresvant."

Lauren thought for a moment and said, "Tresvant. Tresvant. I know that name. There was a man in the auction market that people called by that name."

"Yes, that's him, Walker Tresvant, and he's married to Monsieur Bouvier's sister.

She stopped walking and looked Aubrey in the eyes. "Are you saying Monsieur Bouvier is married?"

"That's what I'm saying."

Totally astonished, she said, "Does she know about him?"

Aubrey was so full of glee he could barely contain himself. "Yes, she knows all about him and his *unusual tastes*, Lauren."

Befuddled, she shook her head and they started walking toward the library again. "Do they have children?"

"My, my, my, suddenly you are full of questions," he said, laughing. "There are children, yes. But they don't belong to Beaumont."

Intrigued, she had to have all the spicy details now. "So the children don't have the Bouvier name?"

Aubrey's smile bubbled to the surface. "Hold on now. I didn't say that. The children have the Bouvier name."

Absolutely hooked now, she had to know the intricacies of the inexplicable yarn that filled her ears and danced in her mind, making her gluttonous for more particulars.

She said, "You simply must tell me how that can be if the children are not Monsieur Bouvier's."

Laughing heartily now, he said, "But they are Monsieur Bouvier's children."

She stopped walking and gently turned him so that he faced her. She needed to see him, look into his eyes, and get all there was. There seemed to be a wealth of information that eluded her; information that he doled out bit by bit, like he had her on a leash, controlling her more with each mouth-watering revelation.

Thirsty for more, she said, "Aubrey, you are a cruel man. You lead me to a spring of cool, fresh water . . . let me look at it, but you only allow me to wet my lips. Come on now, explain that to me. Tell me the whole story. Let me drink."

"Okay, okay, I'll tell you. Monsieur Bouvier has a younger brother named Tristan. You get it now?"

Barely letting him finish his sentence, she said quickly, "You mean his brother is the father of their children?"

She thought of Captain Rutgers at that moment and wondered how often siblings wreck marriages because they don't have the discipline to say no to their passions. She remembered the heartbreaking story he finally told her about his brother Jonah. At first he denied that he had a wife or family. But after spending so much time with her in his quarters, reading, writing, and discussing a myriad of subject matter, he revealed all, just as Amir said he would. She won him over, and truth be told, he won her over a little, too, though she would never admit it.

Aubrey nodded.

She was in heaven now, yet she wasn't satisfied. She wanted it all. She wanted every morsel of the enchanting meal he was serving her.

"How many children do they have?"

As much as Lauren was intrigued by the tale, Aubrey was more intrigued telling it. Everyone at Bouvier Hill knew what was going on and pretended they didn't. Lauren, on the other hand, didn't know anything. To her it was fresh gossip. Her enthusiasm made telling an old story seem exciting and new.

Unable to contain the unfettered elation he felt churning within, he smiled broadly and said, "Four."

"Four? Well, where are they?"

"Visiting relatives in Tallahassee."

"Tallahassee? Where's that?"

"A place called Florida."

"Where's that?"

"A long way from here."

Curious, she wanted to know as much as she could about the Bouvier family. Any information she obtained could be useful in wrecking the family, or securing her release. She was fine with either scenario.

Captain Rutgers had told her she could earn her freedom. She wanted that, and a measure of revenge. As far as she was concerned, she and Amir weren't supposed to be in North America or on the Isle of Santo Domingo. In her quest for revenge, she had conveniently forgotten that she had left Adesola and run away with his younger brother.

She said, "Okay, so, Tristan doesn't want children of his own?"

"He has children of his own."

"I meant with his own wife."

"I know. That's what I meant, too, Lauren."

She thought about what he had just said, and it all began to become clear. Having figured out the answer wasn't good enough. She had to hear it from the man who seemed to have all the answers and knew all the inside information about the family who now owned her.

She said, "Wait a minute. What are you saying?"

"You know what I'm saying."

She shook her head. It made no logical sense. The man who owned her didn't like women, he liked men. And he was fine with his younger brother not only having sex with his wife, but producing children with her as well.

"So, Monsieur Bouvier is fine with all of this?"

"Yes. It works out for everyone. But only the people in this house are supposed to know about it. It's a huge secret. Whatever you do, don't ever repeat it. It would ruin the Bouvier family."

"Sounds like it's already ruined to me, Aubrey."

"Just remember, nobody's perfect . . . including you. Ready to meet Mrs. Bouvier?"

She smiled and said, "Sure. Why not?"

Chapter 39

"I'm sure we're going to get along famously."

Aubrey opened the French doors that served as an entrance to the library. The room was as magnificent as it was large, easily fifty square feet. The marble floors were breathtaking. The ceiling was high and offered thick wooden arches throughout. In the middle of the room sat a long, stained-oak table with five chairs on either side and two at both ends. Several couches and a few smaller tables filled in the center of the room. Built-in bookshelves lined both sides of the room and threatened to touch the ceiling. Stained glass surrounded by brass chandeliers hung from the ceiling in a perfect line. Lamps with the same design as the chandeliers were on the tables and walls.

Tristan and Cadence Bouvier were sitting on one of the couches, chatting like long-lost lovers. When they heard the door open, they stopped talking and synchronously swiveled their heads to see who was interrupting their limited time together. They were careful to keep sufficient distance between them, just in case someone entered unannounced; this made it easier to conceal what everyone on the plantation and beyond already knew.

Tristan and Cadence were approaching their fortieth birthdays, and they were still a good-looking pair. Although Tristan and Beaumont were blood brothers, they looked more like stepbrothers. Tristan was much taller than Beaumont and strikingly handsome, which was why Cadence, a pretty, petite, buxom blonde, wanted to marry him instead. They were instantly attracted to each other the moment Beaumont introduced them. They would have married, but the bulk of the Bouvier fortune would be left to the eldest son when their father died. Besides, Beaumont was a far better businessman. Tristan was an empty suit. He looked good, but he lacked substance and a sense of responsibility and dependability. For those reasons, he and Cadence made a good match.

Cadence Bouvier was a renaissance woman. She was the first of six brothers and sisters, and was used to controlling everything and everyone. Beaumont had been the same, except he was a man, and that little distinction gave him the upper hand in their male-dominated society. His obvious homosexuality rendered her feminine wiles impotent; refusing his sexual advances—not that there were many to begin with—left her feeling totally unnecessary.

Beaumont was the only man she had ever met who had everything together. When her father-in-law died and left everything to him, he redecorated the entire house without so much as a word from her. He didn't even accept her opinion; when she offered it, he told her that her taste in décor was reminiscent of a brothel. Bouvier Manor was a place for heads of state, not lonely men looking for ladies of the evening.

He was even a better cook than she. His self-sufficiency made it easy to start an affair with his younger, irresponsible brother. Besides, the marriage was more of a merger of two rich families who wanted to solidify their fortunes. Even though Cadence's family had money, she was a woman, and the money and the business were left to the men.

She thought she had found her place in life when she realized that Tristan needed her. He was a boy in a man's body. His wife, Christine, thought he was the catch of a lifetime, being a Bouvier. But in truth, Cadence ran Tristan's household, not him. She was his counselor, his confidant, and his consort. She influenced every major decision he made. She decided where they would live, made sure all his bills were paid on time, and told him how to discipline his children. Beaumont would not allow her to run his house, so she ran Tristan's.

To this day, Tristan's wife did not know how much Cadence loathed her. She had the man Cadence wanted but could never have, unless Beaumont died and left her everything. There was no way he'd leave Tristan anything of significance—at least that's what she thought.

"Mrs. Bouvier," Aubrey began, "this is Lauren Renee. She just arrived today, and she says she has a talent for both making and designing clothing."

"Really?" Cadence said and raised her right brow. "Judging by her current appearance, she must have a talent for looking like something the cat dragged in." She looked at Tristan. "What do you think?"

"Oh, I don't know, Cadence. Perhaps you should give her a chance. With all the men doing all the women's work around here, what else is she going to do, work in the cane fields? She's far too delicate a creature for that kind of manual labor."

"Perhaps you're right." She looked at Lauren again. "Where are you from? Judging by your accent, I suspect you're from the Isle of Santo Domingo. Am I right?"

"Nigeria," she said, looking at the floor like Rutgers had taught her.

He had told her that the Southern white woman was insanely jealous of good-looking quadroons and octoroons because white men couldn't get enough of them. While Lauren was neither quadroon nor octoroon, she was fair-skinned and she was beautiful. Her eyes alone were enough to mesmerize any heterosexual male.

"Aubrey, are you serious?" she nearly screamed. "Even if she were the best couturier in New Orleans, she has no idea what we wear here."

"May I speak, Mrs. Bouvier?" Lauren said.

"Speak, child."

"I've been making clothes for more than ten years, designing them for about six years. I'm a fast learner. Show me your designs and I'm sure I can come up with something you'll like."

Cadence liked her right off; she was confident for such a young girl. But she didn't want to let on. Sternly, she asked, "How old are you?"

"Almost seventeen, Mrs. Bouvier."

"Sixteen, huh? Going on thirty, I suspect. Am I right?"

"I don't know what you mean, Mrs. Bouvier."

"Sure you do, Lauren. That's why I like you. You know when to talk and when to keep your mouth shut. Not many women know how to successfully combine the two. You might just work out.

"I have a clothing store in town, and there's an octoroon ball this fall. Tomorrow, I'll see if you're half as good as you *think* you are."

"Thank you, Mrs. Bouvier. You won't regret this."

"I better not." She looked at the torn sleeve again. "So, what happened there?"

Silence.

"Hmpf. I see. Well . . . you two run along now. We were in the middle of something when you barged in."

Smiling devilishly, Tristan said, "I'd like to know what happened to that dress, Lauren. I'd like to know who tore it. Was it my dear brother Beaumont? Was his manhood attempting to reassert itself? I simply refuse to believe that Aubrey or any of the other men of the house would touch you. And I certainly don't believe you, being a designer, would rip such a fine dress. You have no reason to."

Silence.

Hearing nothing from either of them, Cadence said, "You two run along now. I'll see you tomorrow, Lauren. I'm sure we're going to get along famously."

Chapter 40

"What, nigga!"

The grounds of Bouvier Hill seemed to go on forever. Aubrey thought it best to start at the sugarcane fields and then work their way back to the big house. They had been walking the grounds for hours, it seemed. Lauren Renee had been to the edge of the property and had seen the mighty Mississippi River in all of its glory. She had seen the field slaves working feverishly as the blazing evening sun beat down upon them.

The men, women, and children were drenched in sweat; nevertheless, they sang Negro spirituals, which gave them a rhythm. When the field slaves saw Aubrey and Renee, they stopped working momentarily and looked upon them with disdain. Having expressed their displeasure with seeing Aubrey and the new girl, they went back to work.

They spent a significant portion of their time at the sugar house, where the slaves processed the sugar. Aubrey explained that the average sugar plantation was worth about two hundred thousand dollars. He went on to tell her that a cotton plantation of equal size and personnel was only worth half that. Bouvier Hill pulled in more than eight hundred thousand dollars a year. Only the Tresvant plantation rivaled it, bringing in six hundred thousand yearly.

She had seen the dilapidated slave quarters, seen its dirt floors, its inadequate doors and windows, and the poorly designed furniture some of them had. It became clear to her that the slaves were highly undervalued; that the big house, the sugar house, and the stables were the prizes of Bouvier Hill. The product and the animals were treated significantly better than those who made it possible for the other.

When she looked back on it all, she remembered the one night she and Captain Rutgers spent on the Isle of Santo Domingo. She remembered how angry the black men were who attacked the Torvells and how eager they were to destroy everything, how they set the isle ablaze in their indignation. She realized that the right spark at the right time on Bouvier Hill might result in the same revolution; only this time, the field slaves would have an advocate in the big house.

She knew she had to find someone she could trust from among those who did not live in the big house. She knew she had to be extremely careful whom she picked, because it could mean her life if she chose unwisely. The man she chose would have to be intelligent and fearless if they were to mount an organized takeover.

On the trail back to the big house, Aubrey said, "Are you tired, Lauren?"

"A little," she said. "Do we have much more to see?"

"We've got one last stop," he said like he would rather avoid it. "One last *man* to see."

"What's the matter, Aubrey? You look like you don't want to go where we're going," she said, secretly hoping the man they were about to meet would fill the requirements she sought.

Aubrey thought about Joshua, the man to whom he was about to introduce Lauren. His body stiffened, preparing for whatever rude remarks would be hurled their way.

"Do I strike you as a rude man, Lauren?"

She noticed how different he looked, solemn, frowning, taut. "No, but you seem so uneasy right now."

"That's because we're going to see Joshua."

"And . . . I take it you don't like Joshua?"

"It's the other way around. I don't dislike anyone, Lauren. He doesn't like *us*. Any of *us*."

She thought she understood perfectly. She thought it was the same problem that Herman Torvell had explained to her about field slaves and house servants.

She said, "You mean the men in the big house?"

"Yes."

"Why not?" she asked with genuine curiosity. "What's the problem?"

Aubrey sighed. He was so sick of having to hide who he was or to justify being a lover of men. If Monsieur Bouvier weren't wealthy and didn't have the power to destroy lives, the authorities could have come on Bouvier Hill and taken them all to prison and then hanged them. Sodomy was against the law.

He rolled his eyes and huffed, "Joshua doesn't like our manner of speech, and he doesn't like our tastes, which conflict with his."

"Oh, you mean he doesn't like the idea of the men in the big house choosing other men and not women? Is that what you mean, Aubrey?"

"Yes, that's exactly what I mean. And Louis' constant advances don't make it any easier on any of us. I am who I am, Lauren, and I wouldn't have it any other way. Men like me on nearly any other plantation would be killed for our tastes. Here, I'm safe, free to be who I want to be; free to enjoy those things that both please and satisfy my need to be with those who share my tastes. Much like you, I suppose, preferring men rather than women, right?"

"Just one man, Aubrey," she said sweetly. "Only one man has my heart."

"That would be Amir, I trust."

"Yes. Amir."

"I very much would one day like to meet this Amir. He sounds like a wonderful fellow to be sure. Are you sure of his tastes?"

She glared at him. "I am."

"One never knows. You should keep an open mind about these things, dear girl. The pleasures of the flesh are truly unsearchable. There is no limit to the heights one's imagination can soar to. But I speak of things that are beyond your comprehension. You are but a child in a woman's body. You cannot know such things, because you are a virgin and have known neither man nor woman."

"There is but one man I want to know, and his name is—"

"Amir. I got it," he said with a short laugh. "Well, we're here."

She looked to the left and saw a rather robust black man striking iron with a steel mallet. The sound pinged over and over. His arms were a thick mass of rippling muscle, expanding and contracting each time he raised the hammer and lowered it forcefully against the iron shoe he was shaping.

Keeping a comfortable distance between them, Aubrey called out when the hammer was being raised, "Joshua!"

Joshua didn't bother turning around. He had heard that Aubrey and the latest addition to their little family were walking the grounds.

"What, nigga!"

Aubrey looked at Lauren and breathed exasperatedly. Then he whispered, "You see why I avoid this place?"

Lauren remained quiet and listened to the exchange between the men, paying strict attention to their every movement, so she could gauge who Joshua was.

"Joshua," Aubrey began again, his tone sophisticated and erudite. "Dear sir, I would very much like you to meet Lauren Renee. She arrived a few hours ago. Could you please stop what you're doing and turn around and make her acquaintance?"

"I'm busy, nigga! I don't have no time to meet some new house nigga wench!"

Chapter 41

"Hold your horses, nigga!"

Lauren Renee Bouvier started to walk over to Joshua, but Aubrey put his hand on her shoulder to stop her. He shook his head. She ignored Aubrey and went over to where Joshua was working, wondering with every step if he could be the one ally she would need when the time came for the uprising.

He was certainly big and strong enough, she thought. He was certainly defiant enough; but did he have the intelligence and wisdom and patience necessary to mount an insurrection that could grow and turn New Orleans into a conflagration of inexorable heat and smoke? That was the question.

She stood in front of him and hypnotized him with her eyes. For what seemed like five minutes, there was no sound, only quiet and breathing remained. Now, this was a man, she could tell. Only a man would look at her like she was a goddess, like she was the goddess of goddesses.

Only a man would lose his mind and eventually his heart by simply looking at her. Only a man would be weakened by such a gorgeous sight of exquisite beauty.

She thought Aubrey, being a different kind of male, knew nothing of what was passing between them without words, yet he did know, for he had experienced it with the men in the big house of Bouvier Hill.

"Hello. I'm Lauren Renee," she said and offered him her hand. "Happy to make your acquaintance."

Joshua's throat went dry in an instant. He was so lost in her eyes that he couldn't speak. He swallowed hard in an attempt to take command of his larynx. When he finally regained control of his gaping mouth, he could only manage one word miserly word. Unable to keep himself from smiling, he offered a low, breathy "Hi."

He put down the mallet, pulled off the glove from his right hand, wiped it on his pants leg, and took her hand. His hand was incredibly large and swallowed hers whole. He kept holding it, kept shaking it, beaming all the while.

Lauren searched his eyes, looking for his heart. In them, she hoped to find what truth lay behind them. She was looking for a warrior's spirit; a spirit that was strong, precise, and valiant. She was looking for a warrior's heart of conviction and commitment; one that would not only dare to make a plan of revolution, but one that would actually implement that which was diagramed. She was looking for a warrior's heart of wisdom; someone who not only knew how to keep his mouth shut about surreptitious schemes, but who could discern hearts and find others like himself. She didn't know if she had found it in Joshua, but in due time, she would know his heart, as she could see that through one simple introduction, he was hers to do with as she willed. How far he would be willing to go would take time to know.

Aubrey watched them closely, trying to discern if the newest Bouvier was dangerous; if she was friend or foe. He didn't know for sure at that point, but judging by the way her beauty enraptured his enemy, she could, if not deterred, become a problem for Bouvier Hill, and consequently, himself. He watched them communicate without words for a few more moments, studying them reflectively, trying to sense any hint of danger in the form of rebellion. He detected none and assumed that it was a primitive case of reciprocated attraction, nothing more.

Aubrey cleared his throat. "Uh, Lauren . . . we really ought to be getting back to Bouvier Manor, dear."

In a microsecond, Joshua's face became a maze of contortions. He shot a hot glare at Aubrey and said, "Hold your horses, nigga! What be the rush? The woman just got here."

In a demure tone, Aubrey offered a fake laugh and said, "Uh, well . . . she still has to settle in. I have much to show her still. You understand, don't you?"

Joshua picked up the mallet, walked up to Aubrey, and pointed it in his face. "No, I don't understand, fancy pants, and neither do you." He put the mallet on Aubrey's chest and shoved him with it. "What be the rush? She ain't goin' nowhere. She gon' be here from now on . . . and you rushin' around like she got a ship waitin' for her in the harbor or somethin'. She gon' be here fo' the duration, up yonder in the big house with the rest of you fancy-talkin' niggas, ain't she?"

Aubrey took a step backward each time Joshua pushed the heavy mallet into his chest.

"Oh, Joshua, honestly. Do you *really* have to be so obnoxious all the time? That's why I didn't want to come down here. I just knew you'd find a way to start something."

Joshua shoved hard with the mallet and backed him up farther. "Well, if you knew I was gon' start somethin', whatcha come down here fo'?"

"I didn't want to come down here. It was on the way to the big house, and Lauren wanted to meet you. Believe me, if it were up to me, we would have avoided this wretched place like the bubonic plague."

"Like the *what*?"

Aubrey rolled his eyes. "The bubonic plague. The Black Death. Are you so ignorant that you've never heard of it?"

"*Ignorant*?" Joshua took a couple of threatening steps toward Aubrey. "Don't make me bus' yo' head wide open with this here mallet, hear?"

"Uh, Joshua," Lauren interrupted.

She had seen what she came to see. Joshua was indeed her man. He lacked wisdom and temperament, but he had a warrior's heart. His fury would have to be curtailed until such time that it could be unleashed. He either didn't know or didn't care that Aubrey had the ear of Monsieur Bouvier. At Bouvier's command, he could be beaten to death, or within an inch of his life, and then where would she be? She had to bring the rift between the men to a peaceful end and build trust with Joshua in the immediate future.

"I did want to meet you and the rest of our people. Now that I have, I better go. We'll talk again, I'm sure. Like you said, there's no ship waiting for me in the harbor. I'm not going anywhere for a very long time."

Joshua turned around and faced Lauren. Smiling, he said, "I look forward to seeing you again, pretty lady. You stop on by any time you like." Then he looked at Aubrey. "But leave fancy pants at the big house next time, ya hear?"

Lauren smiled.

They started toward the big house.

"Oh, and *fancy*," Joshua began, "I got somethin' tuh say to Louis. Tell 'im I know he be watchin' me when he think I don't see 'im. But I sees him, sittin' up there on that there terrace, naked as a jaybird, touchin' his self. You tell 'im if he come near again, I'ma take this here mallet o' mine and bus' his head wide open, ya hear? That's goes for the rest of them Romans in the big house too. All of ya pre-verted.

"And pretty lady, whateva you do, don't you trust them fancy-talkin' niggas up there on the hill."

Chapter 42

"Know this, child: Monsieur Bouvier is my security."

"**C**an I ask you a question, Aubrey?" Lauren said as they neared the big house.

"Anything, dear girl."

"What's the bubonic plague?"

Somberly, Aubrey said, "Oh, that bit of information that eluded our good friend and resident blacksmith was a disease that killed lots of people about four hundred years ago in Europe."

"Europe, hmm," Lauren repeated, remembering that Rutgers had told her he was from Belgium.

Sensing she had more questions, he said, "Don't hold back, Lauren. Please, continue. Let me hear your thoughts. I very much want us to be friends. We will be in the big house together, you know? So please, don't hold back now. What do you want to know?"

"Well, I'm wondering how you know such things," she began. "If the bubonic plague happened four hundred years ago in Europe, a three-month journey from this place, how would you know about it?"

"Lauren Renee Bouvier,"—Aubrey smiled broadly—"I perceive that somewhere inside you lies a perceptive intellect. Tell me, dear girl, what makes you ask? Curiosity? Or do you have a burning desire for knowledge?"

"Oh, Aubrey, don't make such a big deal of it," she said, knowing in her heart that Aubrey could be counted on to conspire against the best interests of his own people, much like Herman Torvell. She wrapped her arm around his as before and laid her head on his shoulder as they walked along the path to the big house. "It's just a simple question."

Aubrey stopped their casual stroll and looked deep into her eyes. Then he reached out his hand, lifted her chin, and said, "Can I trust you, Lauren Renee Bouvier?"

"We're friends, aren't we?" she said as sincerely as she could, knowing she could never be friends with a man like him; a man she considered a traitor.

"Okay, I'll trust you then," he began. "Remember when we were in the library?"

"Yes, of course."

"Remember all those books lining the shelves on the walls?"

"Yes."

"Monsieur Bouvier taught me how to read, and he lets me read them."

"Really?"

"But no one outside the big house can ever know this. Why . . . if it ever got out that we can read, they would kill us."

"Why? And who is we?"

"The men in the big house. We can all read."

"Oh, okay. But why would they kill you?"

"Because they might get it in their heads that we would turn against them and side with the field slaves. When one learns to read, writing is within one's grasp. We could write passes for slaves to help them escape plantation life to the North. Some slaves have done this and have paid with their very lives for doing so."

Lauren pretended to be astounded by the secret revelations. She had already considered much of what he was saying when she was aboard the Windward. She had learned from Captain Rutgers that older men relished the idea of teaching young girls things that men think are important. So she let him run his mouth, listening closely, hanging on to every word, like he was teaching her the world was not square, but round.

She said, "Can you teach me to read, Aubrey?"

"I can and I will, but you must never let Cadence and Tristan know of it. And if you are ever caught reading, you must not tell them I taught you. You must take it to your grave, or we will all pay the grim reaper's toll."

"Why can't either of them know?"

"Because neither of them can be trusted; especially Cadence. If they thought they could get away with it, they'd kill Monsieur Bouvier and take over the plantation. That's what I think anyway. He doesn't need either of them."

"He doesn't?"

"No, he doesn't. They need him because he has all the money. Unfortunately, we, the men of the house, need him too, but for different reasons. We need Monsieur Bouvier because he makes it possible for men of our tastes to exist."

"So Cadence doesn't know you can read."

"That's Mrs. Bouvier to you. Never ever call her Cadence," he said sternly. After scolding her, he continued, "She knows I can read. She also knows I run the plantation and I do the books. I know everything.

"Monsieur Bouvier trusts me with everything, and I dare not take that trust lightly. Why do you think a man of my superior intellect chooses to live in this manner when I could run my own plantation like Monsieur Tresvant and the other free people of color in New Orleans?"

He didn't wait for an answer.

"Know this, child: Monsieur Bouvier is my security. Without him, Cadence would take over in a heartbeat, and her first order of business would be to rid herself of the homosexual infestation within the walls of Bouvier Manor. We would not survive among the field workers. They hate us.

"And so she will try to align herself with you because you are female first and black second, not the other way around. I suppose if the men of Bouvier Hill were more to her liking, men who would ravage her sweetly, you would then be black first and female second in her eyes. Now, she probably sees you as a potential ally."

Hmm, so there's a war going on inside the house. I'll make sure they stay divided and destroy them all. Then when the time is right, Joshua and the other field hands will swoop in, and we'll take our freedom back.

"Okay, Aubrey. What do you need me to do?"

"Tell me everything she tells you."

Confused, she asked, "Why would she tell me anything important?"

"She won't at first. But after a while, when she trusts you, she'll confide in you. All you have to do is listen and report everything back to me, okay? Can you do that?"

So you want me to be your spy, huh, Aubrey? You want me to be your stooge? You'll be my stooge, Aubrey. So will Cadence and the rest of you. I'm a survivor with a warrior's heart. I will prevail.

She hugged him and then looked into his eyes. "Yes, Aubrey, I sure can. You can trust me."

Chapter 43

Sixty-nine

A chilling scream echoed off the corridor walls of the house on Bouvier Hill early the next morning, and woke up all its inhabitants. There were only two women in the house, so when Lauren opened her bedroom door and entered the hallway, it didn't take the men long to figure out who was screaming.

The Bouvier mansion was three stories high and had a large wine cellar beneath it. The men of the house and Lauren slept on the third floor. While Beaumont and Cadence did not sleep together or in the same bedroom, they did share the second floor. Beaumont slept in a bedroom on one side of the house, and Cadence slept in the last bedroom on the other side of the hall, far from him.

There were two ways to get to the second floor stairs, so when Lauren saw the men racing down the staircase near her room, she followed quickly to see what had happened. She saw Cadence standing at Beaumont's door, staring inside. Her face looked like every drop of blood had drained from it.

The men rushed inside to see what had happened, but Lauren just looked at Cadence's face, which mesmerized her. She had never seen anyone so completely shocked by what they had seen.

Aubrey was the last one to arrive at Beaumont's bedroom. He walked in, gasped, and said, "Oh God, no!"

All of a sudden, all the men were crying uncontrollably, and Lauren still hadn't looked in there. She still hadn't seen what everyone had seen. The unrestrained anguish that came from somewhere deep within the men beckoned her, calling her into the room as if by her new name.

She left Cadence in the hallway and entered the room. What she saw in there topped everything she'd seen since the night she stepped over her mother and crawled out the open window to meet Amir.

She thought she had seen it all. She had seen Amir kill several men in a matter of seconds. She had seen men chained in the cargo hold of a slave ship and smelled their putrid filth, which made her heave. She had seen a man beaten to death with a bullwhip then tossed over the side like his life didn't matter. She had seen Captain Rutgers drag a woman by her hair to his quarters and witnessed her brutal rape. She had seen man-eating sharks devour a man, a woman, and even a little girl. At the time, that had topped everything, which was why she could watch a slave having his skin peeled from the auction block without looking away.

What she had seen previously was nothing compared

to what was entering through her twin portals now. She put her hand over her mouth to keep from screaming and vomiting, in that order, yet never once did she turn away. It was like someone's powerful hands were holding her head in place, forcing her to see what no one should ever have to see. What she saw was beyond frightening, beyond tragic, beyond brutal. What she saw were the acts of an evil mind. Only an evil mind could do that to another human being and hope to get away with it.

Then she saw something familiar and nearly jumped out of her skin. The steel mallet that Joshua had been using the previous day was lying on the floor. Blood and hair was stuck to its head. She looked at the bed again and saw the remains of Beaumont and Louis. They were both naked, lying in a sixty-nine position, as pools of their blood intermingled on the bed and dripped on the floor. Their plows had been cut off and stuck in each other's mouths.

Although none of the men said a word, the identity of the person who had committed the vile act could be read on their faces. Only one name registered—Joshua.

Chapter 44

"Before we kill him, let's turn him into a Roman!"

Lauren saw blood everywhere she looked. It was on the headboard, on the walls, the floor, and all over them. It looked like Joshua had come into the house when he knew everyone would be asleep and pummeled both men to death with his steel mallet. He had done a real number on them. Their skulls were caved in. They looked like every bone in their faces had been shattered; teeth were all over the room. She watched Aubrey pull their plows out of their mouths, which left them looking like jack-o-lanterns long before Halloween.

She looked into the faces of the housemen. Grief was about to consume them, not only because Monsieur Bouvier and Louis had been killed. It was the manner in which they met their end that filled them with rage.

The instant the housemen saw the steel mallet, they tried and convicted Joshua without the benefit of a courtroom. And now they were about to go looking for him to dispense the justice they thought he deserved.

When they filed past Cadence, she did nothing to delay or stop them. She stepped out of their way, giving them her approval without saying a single word.

First they stormed into the stable looking for him. When they didn't find him there, they grabbed a rope and made a noose of it. Next they went to the slave quarters. Being the plantation stud, they thought he was making time with one of the women.

Lauren went along with them, hoping they wouldn't find him, hoping they wouldn't cross paths with the man she thought would be her deliverer. If they did see Joshua, they were going to kill him on the spot. They weren't going to ask questions. They were going to tear him to pieces for what he had done to their master and their friend.

On the way, she heard one of the housemen say, "Let's cut that nigga's plow off first and stick it in *his* mouth!"

Another, who had the steel mallet, said, "I'ma bash in his skull first so he can see how it feels!"

Still another said, "He calls us Romans because of our tastes! Before we kill him, let's turn him into a Roman!"

Another said, "Yeah! All of us too! One at a time! All night long!"

Aubrey was the only voice of reason in the chaotic situation. He said, "Men of Bouvier Hill, let's not lose our heads over this. This is a matter for the law. I'll go to town and get the constable, and we'll turn Joshua over to him."

One of the men said, "Go and get him, Aubrey. I can't

guarantee there'll be much left of him by the time you return."

The housemen kicked in door after door, only to find each residence empty. Bouvier Hill had more than two hundred slaves, so there were plenty of shacks to search. And search they did, relentlessly, growing more angry, but determined to find the man who killed their benefactor so brutally.

There were only a few shacks left to search. Approaching one, they heard the sound of fever-pitched intimacy. They had Joshua, and he was naked; being nude and doing the same things Beaumont and Louis were doing was an unexpected bonus.

They kicked in the door and rushed over to the naked couple wildly copulating. They pulled the man out of the woman and had nearly beaten him to death as the woman protested before they realized they had the wrong man.

The housemen grew more frustrated, but were unrepentant for almost killing the wrong man. They had gotten a measure of satisfaction from the assault. As far as they were concerned, what they had done to him by mistake sent a strong message to any other would-be murderers who gave serious consideration to coming within reach of the big house while they slept comfortably in the beds.

The man had been beaten so severely that they didn't bother asking him any questions about Joshua's whereabouts. They did, however, interrogate the woman with the same ferocious behavior, kicking and punching her until she bled.

"Where's Joshua?" one of the men yelled.

"I don't know! I don't know!" she screamed.

They punched her and kicked her a few more times.

She looked up at the men beating her. Blood trickled down her nose and mouth. "I swear I don't know where he is! He stopped visiting me a long time ago. He ain't been by to see me in months, so I found myself another man!"

When they told her why they were looking for Joshua, her reaction to hearing about the death of Monsieur Bouvier was one of genuine surprise. Though she would never weep over any of their deaths, she didn't wish them any ill will either.

Chapter 45

"His life hangs in the balance."

The housemen didn't stop looking for Joshua until it was dark, and only after they had searched the entire plantation and the surrounding area twice. Several of them wanted to light torches and continue the search, but Aubrey convinced them that Joshua had somehow found out that they were looking for him and fled for his life.

They had decided to call it a night when they heard someone knocking. Aubrey went to the door and opened it. He saw Walker Tresvant, his wife and Monsieur Bouvier's sister, Marie-Elise, and a regiment of armed French soldiers. In their haste to find and deliver swift justice to Joshua, they had not contacted the garrison commander as the law required.

Aubrey fixed his eyes on Monsieur Tresvant. "We were just about to contact you, dear sir. There's been a tragic death in the Bouvier family."

Walker barged in, pushing Aubrey out of the way with

his shoulder as he passed. "We know all about it," he said roughly. "Where's the body? We want to it see right now!"

Marie-Elise didn't bother acknowledging Aubrey as she walked past him. She didn't even look at him. Behind her was a man in uniform. He walked in too.

"Monsieur Tresvant, I don't mean to trouble you on a night such as this, but who shall I say this gentleman is?"

"I'm Lieutenant Avery. Troy Avery. The commandant is away on business and left me in charge. I'm here to investigate the murder of one Beaumont Bouvier."

"Lieutenant Avery," Aubrey began, "there's no need to investigate. We know who killed Monsieur Bouvier."

Lieutenant Avery was about to respond when Walker said, "Do you, now?" He parted his jacket and put his hands on his hips. "I can tell you this much: it wasn't Joshua."

Aubrey's face shattered. His mouth fell open, but no words exited.

Walker stepped to him and got right in his face, their noses almost touching. "That's right, fancy pants; it wasn't Joshua. And since it wasn't Joshua, that means one of you good-for-nothing Romans did the deed. My considerable money's on you, Aubrey."

Aubrey took a few steps backward and said, "Me? Surely you jest, dear sir. Why would *I* kill Monsieur Bouvier? He was my . . ." His words trailed off.

Marie-Elise offered a disgusted frown and said, "My dear brother was your what?"

Aubrey responded with loud silence. He knew he couldn't say what they were all pretending not to know.

The truth acknowledged and death were one and the same.

Lieutenant Avery remained quiet and observed Aubrey's reaction to Walker's stinging accusation.

"I'll say it since you won't!" Walker screamed. "He was your lover, right? Right? Go on . . . tell us. He was your lover, right? Say it!"

"Walker Tresvant, what's the meaning of this intrusion?" Cadence said when she entered the foyer.

Lauren and the housemen listened attentively.

"I think you know the meaning, Cadence," Marie-Elise said with rancor. She knew of Cadence's affair with her younger brother Tristan, and it angered her to see her acting as if she was in love with Beaumont. The marriage had been a sham from the start. It was a marriage of convenience and for the consolidation of power. Beaumont needed a wife to cover up his homosexuality, and Cadence married Beaumont in an effort to gain power. She had assumed that Beaumont was weak because he was effeminate. When she found out that he wasn't weak and that she was expected to behave like any other married woman, she thought she had been tricked and began to loathe him.

"I most certainly do not," Cadence said. "My dear husband—"

"Your *dear* husband?" Marie-Elise questioned, disrupting her sister-in-law in mid-sentence. "Don't pretend to love my brother now that he's gone to meet his maker."

"What . . . on . . . earth are you talking about, Marie-Elise?" Cadence asked. "What's this all about?"

"It's about money and property, Cadence!" Walker shouted.

"Bouvier money, Cadence," Marie-Elise added, backing her husband's play. They had carefully planned this little scene before leaving Chateau Tresvant.

"My dear husband was murdered today and his body isn't even cold yet, and you two come here screaming at me about money and property? Are you two insane?"

"I'm sure his body is quite cold by now," Marie-Elise said sarcastically. "Come to think of it, it's been cold where you're concerned from the beginning. Isn't that right?"

Cadence slapped her face so hard that it left a hand print on her cheek. She screamed, "How dare you!"

Marie-Elise was stunned by the sudden stinging blow. When she had been slapped, she returned the favor with the back of her hand. A fight was about to break out, but the men separated the women before any more blows were thrown.

"Lieutenant," Walker shouted, "are you going to stand there stone-faced while she assaults and insults my wife?"

"Let's all calm down and keep our wits," Avery said calmly. "Where's the body? I want to see it. Until I see a body, there is no official death."

"He's upstairs in his room," Cadence said. She looked at Walker. "If you care anything about your wife, don't let her go up there and see him like that."

Aubrey said, "May I ask how you know for certain that Joshua did not kill Monsieur Bouvier?"

"I know he didn't kill him because he was at my plantation all night with a female I own. If you doubt that, tell me how I know all about the tour you gave Lauren Renee

Bouvier. How do I know her new name if I have not been in contact with Joshua or the girl?"

"That you were in contact with him does not prove he didn't kill Monsieur Bouvier and Louis," Aubrey said. He hated the idea that no one seemed to recognize that there were two murders, not just one. He couldn't help but think that if Louis were a woman and was found in the same condition, everyone would acknowledge both deaths. "He could have killed *them* and then gone over to your plantation to secure an alibi. It only proves that Joshua somehow learned that the men of Bouvier Hill sought to have a word with him. Knowing this, and perhaps fearing for his life, he fled to a place he considered sanctuary."

Lieutenant Avery finally said, "And what do you make of the girl's assertion that the man in question was with her the entire night?"

"What is the penalty for murder, Lieutenant?" Aubrey asked.

"Death by a firing squad," the lieutenant answered without contemplation.

"So then, if you find that he did in fact kill both men, how soon would you carry out the death sentence?"

"Immediately. This very night. This very moment. I brought the soldiers from the garrison for the occasion."

"Again, sir, that is precisely why he lied about his whereabouts," Aubrey said. "His life hangs in the balance."

"There are two flaws in your line of reasoning," the Lieutenant said.

Aubrey raised his eyebrows. "Flaws, sir?"

"Yes, flaws. First, he did not lie about his whereabouts, as you claim. The man was as forthright as one could be. The woman he was with confirms this. Second, if he were worried about the immediacy of death, as you assert, why would he run to a neighboring plantation, see a woman, lie with her, and remain with her all night, knowing full well that he, being a black man and a slave, killed a white man in his own house, in his own bed?"

Chapter 46

"My money's on you, fancy pants."

When Lieutenant Avery refused a second time to acknowledge that Louis was murdered as well, Aubrey wanted to strangle him; nevertheless, he took a deep breath and maintained his composure—his life hung in the balance too. If he let it slip out that he was a Sodomite, it would be all over for him. Instead, he paced the floor back and forth, searching for a solution to support his theories. None came to him.

Avery was right, he thought. If Joshua had killed Beaumont and Louis, it made no sense to run only as far as Chateau Tresvant. That was either the act of an innocent man, or the act of an incredibly stupid man. As much as he hated to admit it, Joshua, for all of his flaws, was far from stupid. That meant someone from the big house may have committed the murders and implicated Joshua. He wondered, as he paced, who would do it? His mind was suddenly flooded with questions.

"You're very well informed, Lieutenant Avery," Aubrey said. "Tell me, how were you able to get such meticulous information, if not from the killer himself? The *murders* were committed sometime last night, yet you are here without an invitation, parceling out specific details."

"The slave you and several other men nearly killed this morning told us everything," Avery said. "Is that true? Did you and the housemen here assault him and the woman he was with?"

Aubrey lowered his eyes, but remained quiet.

Walker said, "It turns out that the slave who told us this knew that Joshua had been sneaking off to my plantation at night for some time now, sporting with one of my servants. He told the man you pummeled this morning all about it, which is why you caught him in bed with a woman that Joshua stopped seeing a long time ago."

Aubrey silenced himself and started pacing the floor again. He knew that he and the other men were in serious trouble now. First, their benefactor was dead and gone, never to return. That left them in the hands of a power-hungry woman who felt slighted by the man she married to get the power she craved. Now she had it, and all the housemen's lives were in her hands.

He believed that if Joshua didn't do it, Tristan and Cadence did, but he couldn't accuse a white woman of killing her own husband, not because he was effeminate, but to garner power. Who would ever believe that? He was desperate now. He had to do something he didn't want to do—accuse Lauren, who he didn't believe for a second had committed the crime. But it was either her or him.

She had only been there a day. He didn't know her that well and owed her no allegiance.

Cadence said, "If Joshua didn't kill Beaumont, who did?"

Lieutenant Avery said, "One of you did it. There can be no doubt."

Aubrey hated himself for what he was about to do, but it had to be done if he and the other men were to live. Without conviction, in a soft, almost inaudible whisper, he served her up to them. "What about Lauren? She just got here. She may have done it."

Lauren frowned when she heard Aubrey implicate her in a brutal double murder. Only yesterday he had said he wanted to be her friend; he wanted her to trust him and build an alliance. He had even asked her to be his spy, so that he could gather information on Cadence. Now he was throwing her to a different form of man-eater. The last words that Joshua had said the day before rang in her mind: "Whateva you do, don't you trust them fancy-talkin' niggas up there on the hill."

"You can't be serious," Lieutenant Avery said.

"I most certainly am serious," Aubrey blurted out angrily. He had to tell it all now. His life depended on it. "Monsieur Bouvier tried to force himself on her yesterday. I can get you the dress he nearly tore off her. Maybe he tried again and was successful the second time. And Louis insulted her moral sensibilities by prancing around her nude like he wanted to violate her as well. She could have waited until he and Louis were most vulnerable and killed them both."

Lieutenant Avery rolled his eyes and said, "For a moment or two, I thought I was talking to a learned intellectual, being a slave notwithstanding. Now, however, I see that you have no reasoning skills whatsoever. I'm told that both men were in bed together, engaging in unlawful, salacious activity.

"I don't believe a girl could do such a thing to two men. Nevertheless, we'll leave no stone unturned. Where's the girl? Bring her out here and let's see if she has the strength to subdue two men."

Lauren stepped out into the foyer when she heard the lieutenant's request. She glared at Aubrey. She was glad she hadn't confided in him. He had sold her out in a matter of minutes to save his own skin. No real warrior would ever put himself before a friend. If she had the steel mallet at that moment, she would have buried it deep inside his head and proudly stood before a firing squad for doing so.

"I'm Lauren, sir."

Lieutenant Avery looked into her eyes and was immediately enraptured by them. After a few seconds of wanton gazing, he looked the girl up and down skeptically. She was rather tall, but he didn't believe for a second that she could have subdued two men and killed them. He kind of laughed and said, "Surely you don't think this delicate flower had the wherewithal to commit this wretched crime."

Aubrey shrugged his shoulders and said, "Well . . . somebody had to have killed them. I can't imagine that any of us did it." He was referring to the housemen, not Cadence.

"Show me where the body is . . . now!" Avery said.

Marie-Elise took Cadence's advice and stayed behind while the housemen, Lauren, Walker, and Avery made their way up to the second floor and into Beaumont's bedroom. They lit several lamps so they could see. Beaumont and Louis remained exactly as they were, in a sixty-nine position. Their plows sat side by side on the nightstand.

Avery looked at Aubrey and said, "Do you still maintain that either Joshua or Lauren here did this?"

Aubrey looked at the floor and without passion said, "I do, sir."

Avery shook his head. "Aubrey, tell me then, if you can, why would Joshua leave the murder weapon that would be easily traced to him, and yet, not flee New Orleans altogether? And if Lauren did this, how was she able to kill them both while they were awake? And if she were able to somehow kill them both in their sleep, does she have the strength it would take to arrange two dead men in such a fashion as this?"

Aubrey said, "Well, someone killed them, sir. Who did it?"

Walker said, "My money's on you, fancy pants."

"Me? Why would I do such a thing? I have nothing to gain. You, on the other hand, do."

Chapter 47

"Take them all out and shoot them."

Walker Tresvant looked at Aubrey. Pity and compassion enveloped him. The man was grasping at straws now. It made no sense. Why would he not only come back to the scene of the crime, but bring a regiment of French soldiers? In order to commit the crime and hope to get away with it, he would have had to have known that Joshua was staying at his plantation that particular night and that he wasn't going back to Bouvier Hill. He would have had to have been able to find his steel mallet in the darkness, as he dare not light a torch and risk attracting the attention of the people he was going to kill. He then would have had to sneak into the mansion, up the stairs, kill Beaumont and Louis without making a sound, and get back out of the mansion without being seen.

Walker ran his hand down his face and said, "Now that we've exonerated two of your suspects, you aim your guns of judgment at me? For what reason would I do this?"

"Money and property. Bouvier money and property. That's what you said downstairs. I submit that you knew about Joshua and your servant all along, didn't you? You waited for the right time, and when you saw him go into your servant's quarters last night, you came over here, grabbed his mallet knowing it would implicate Joshua, killed your brother-in-law, and tried to escape. But Louis saw you, and you had to kill him too to shut him up.

"Then, to cover your tracks and implicate Joshua in the grisly deed, you cut off their plows and stuck them in their mouths, because you knew of Joshua's, and perhaps your own, hatred of our *perceived* inclinations and preferences. If Monsieur Bouvier's will leaves significant money to his sister, you would be in a position to take over Bouvier Hill, which was why you married her in the first place, right Monsieur Tresvant? Isn't that the real reason you came over here? Bringing a regiment of French soldiers and Lieutenant Avery is nothing more than an elaborate ruse to throw suspicion off you and onto other innocent parties. Isn't that so?"

Lieutenant Avery watched Walker closely to see his reaction to Aubrey's accusations. He was unmoved by it—outwardly anyway.

Walker applauded and said, "Touché, Aubrey. Touché. You probably would have made a great attorney, or swordsman. You've managed to implicate two people who could not have done it, so you then accuse the only man with what you think is real motive—money and property. The only problem is that I spent the entire night at Madam Nadine's brothel playing high stakes poker with the mayor and several planters, all of whom will vouch for me.

"Besides, I'm already rich. Why would I risk everything to take over Bouvier Hill; especially since Beaumont, in all likelihood, didn't leave Marie-Elise a dime because of his disdain for me? I have no idea who he left his enormous wealth to. I would think he left his fortune to either his wife or his brother, not my wife.

"Now . . . what do you have to say to that? Who are you going to accuse next? My wife?"

"If you believe that, dear sir, why did you mention money and property when you entered Bouvier Manor?"

"One can always hope. I'd be lying if I said I didn't hope he left Marie-Elise a significant portion of the Bouvier fortune. If we combine our wealth, we could absorb the smaller plantations and become the biggest sugar producers in Louisiana. You do the books, Aubrey, don't you?"

"Yes, sir."

"Then you know it's the right move, right?"

Aubrey nodded.

"Can you think of a good reason why I'd jeopardize the possibility of Tresvant and Bouvier Sugar consolidating?"

Silence filled the room.

"What about . . ." Aubrey thought better of who he was about to accuse and stifled himself.

"What about what, Aubrey?" Walker asked.

"Nothing, sir. I'm at a loss as to who may have committed the murders."

"Come on, man, speak up," Avery said. "We know you know something."

Soberly, Aubrey said, "I've accused three people who

did not commit the murders; I will not accuse a fourth party, sir."

Avery looked at the housemen and Lauren. "None of you heard anything last night? Nothing?"

Silence.

"I'd like to apologize to you, Monsieur Tresvant, and to you, too, Lauren. I suppose I've allowed grief to get the better of me on this tragic day," Aubrey said. "Someone killed the master of this house, and I don't know who. I'm afraid it is one of us. Who else could have found Joshua's mallet in the darkness?"

They all went downstairs. Cadence and Marie-Elise came out of the sitting room to find out what they learned.

Avery said, "Mrs. Bouvier, I'm afraid we're no closer to solving this crime than we were before we went upstairs. One thing we all agree on is that somebody living here killed your husband. My suggestion is that you pick one or two of your niggers and we'll shoot them before we leave. You might get lucky and pick the guilty party, or not, but someone will have paid with their lives for the crime. Or you can hope that someone confesses later. It's up to you. At this point, I can't do any more than that."

"So you want me to pick one of my servants so you can shoot him. And that will solve the crime?"

"It won't solve the crime, Mrs. Bouvier, but it will bring a bit of satisfaction. Pick one that gives you problems. I really don't care. I have other duties to perform at the garrison. The city beckons. We must take our leave. What's it going to be?"

Cadence looked at all the housemen and said, "One of

you killed my husband, and one of you will pay for his death with your own life."

She walked up to each one and looked into their eyes, hoping to find a reason to accuse them by something she saw or thought she saw in them. When she came to Aubrey, she smirked and made sure he saw it, so that he would know that she had orchestrated the whole thing. What was he going to do, cast suspicion on the wife of the deceased; a white woman in mourning, no less, who had just been given authority to have him shot to death?

When she was sure he knew that it was her all along, she said, "Lieutenant Avery, I want to you take Aubrey outside and shoot him in his head."

"No, please, Mrs. Bouvier. I'm innocent," Aubrey said. "I would never do something like this. Not to Monsieur Bouvier. I wouldn't. Please, you must believe me."

Lauren knew what Aubrey knew or at least believed, but she couldn't say either. They had seen Tristan and Cadence talking in the library. They did not want to be disturbed. As far as she was concerned, they were the likely suspects. As much as she wanted to bail Aubrey out, she couldn't. Aubrey was finished at Bouvier Hill, just as he had said the day before. If they didn't believe a black girl could commit the murders, they certainly weren't going to believe a white woman, the wife of the deceased, no less, and her brother-in-law did.

Besides all that, she had only been on the plantation for a day. She didn't know Aubrey. She wasn't about to stick her neck out for any of them. Since Aubrey accused her of killing Monsieur Bouvier, she felt no obligation to say anything about the affair that Mrs. Bouvier was having with Tristan or the children they made together. As far as she was concerned, they killed Beaumont.

To save Aubrey, one of the housemen lied and said, "I did it, Mrs. Bouvier. Aubrey had nothing to do with it."

Then, one by one, all the housemen confessed to the crime none of them committed. They had hoped to forestall Aubrey's execution by adding even more confusion to the mix, but they had all terribly miscalculated Cadence's ruthlessness.

To the series of confessions, Cadence said, "Fine. Take them all out and shoot them in their heads." Their confessions were an unexpected godsend. She was going to get rid of them anyway. Getting rid of the housemen was the only way she would have felt safe sleeping in her own house. "Before you execute them, I want them to dig graves for themselves and for my dearly departed husband. When they finish, shoot them so that they fall into their graves. I'll have the other servants cover them up afterward."

By the time they finished digging their graves, the roosters were crowing and the sun was up. All the slaves were made to watch the execution of the house slaves. Walker Tresvant and Marie-Elise were still there, waiting to see them die. Lauren stood next to Cadence, watching and hoping she wasn't next. The French soldiers lined Aubrey and the others up in front of the graves, seven in all.

"Shall I give them blindfolds, Mrs. Bouvier?" Avery asked.

"No. I want them to see it coming," she said. "They killed Beaumont without mercy. They shall receive the same, without mercy."

"Ready!" Avery called out to his men.

They prepared to fire.

"I didn't kill nobody, Mrs. Bouvier," one of the men shouted. "None of us did!"

"Take aim!" Avery commanded.

"Men of Bouvier Hill," Aubrey said loudly. "We will not whine and will not beg for our lives. We are Romans, and we shall die like the Romans we are."

The housemen stood up straight and stuck out their chests like soldiers.

"Fire!" Avery commanded.

Pow! Pow! Pow! Pow! Pow! Pow!

Their bodies jerked and contorted in response to the bullets that entered them. Some of them grabbed their faces as they fell back into the graves.

"Reload!" Avery shouted.

The men reloaded and stood over the graves.

"Fire!"

Smoke filled the air.

"Reload!"

The men reloaded a second time.

"Fire!"

Chapter 48

"Where's Lauren?"

The previous day's excitement and sadness had kept both Lauren and Cadence up all night. When she finally had the chance to lie down and sleep, all of what had happened to her and the people around her dominated her thoughts. She came to realize that Captain Rutgers was right when he said, "You're about to enter a world where your life has little to no value." Before she was captured and taken aboard the Windward, she had never seen anybody die. She had never been to a funeral, although she had heard of them and what they were for. But in the place called America, murder was a way of life. She realized that in order to survive, she may have to kill or cause the death of someone else, much like Cadence had done.

She wondered how her life would turn out if she behaved like the Dutch and the Americans. She wasn't sure how much more death she could take without killing someone herself. It seemed to be the acceptable way to gain power, and to live, for that matter.

After seeing what Cadence did to Aubrey and the rest of the housemen, she knew the time was coming when she too would kill, as it was becoming a part of her. She could watch men be killed and not be moved by their deaths. She soon began to wonder if she would be consumed by the powerful jaws of death before she had a chance to experience what Aubrey called the unsearchable pleasures of the flesh.

She was alone and she felt isolated, even though New Orleans and Bouvier Hill were populated with people who looked like her. She felt no kinship with them. The loneliness she felt was starting to consume her. The only thing that made her smile was Amir, and that was the Amir that she had met in Dahomey, not the one she left on the Isle of Santo Domingo. That Amir was a shadow of the one she fell in love with and risked all for.

The insurgent Maroons were mounting an impressive offensive when she was whisked away from the Isle of Santo Domingo. They had set a great fire when she saw it last. She didn't know if Amir was dead or alive. His promise to come for her was starting to ring hollow. For a while, she clung to his word as if it were her life's blood, but now, months after they left him there on the burning isle, she was starting to accept that not only was she never going to see her family again, she was never going to see the man she thought was the air she breathed.

For reasons unknown to her, Joshua came to mind. She told herself it was because he reminded her of Amir. That way she could justify her feelings. She could see him pounding the horseshoe, forcing it to become what he wanted it to be. She could see his rippling muscles and wondered if they were as hard as they looked. She remembered the way he looked at her, like he wanted her, like he would do anything in the world to make her his own. Could he protect her from the evil the world was offering? He sure talked like it, she thought, when she remembered the way he pushed Aubrey around.

Then she remembered something Joshua said, a single word he used; one she had never heard before: *nigga.* What did it mean? And was it the same word that she had heard Lieutenant Avery and the Dutchmen on the Windward use when they said "Nigger"? Was it the same word and they pronounced it differently? She didn't know; however, she did know that she couldn't sleep.

She hadn't done any reading since she and Captain Rutgers came ashore. She decided to risk going down to the library to read one of the many books that lined its walls.

Fearing for her life, Lauren had stayed away from Cadence the entire day. With all the housemen dead, the house was incredibly quiet. It was easy to hear movement. When she'd heard Cadence walking, she made sure she went in the opposite direction. She walked up to the closed door of her room and listened for any movement. Hearing none, she carefully turned the knob and opened it.

She listened for Cadence, but heard nothing. On her toes, she crept toward the staircase farthest from Cadence's room and descended the stairs. When she reached the landing to turn the corner, she craned her neck to see in the darkness. Even though Cadence's room was at the other end of the hall, Lauren could see light cutting through the darkness. Her door was half opened.

For a fleeting second, Lauren was about to turn around and go back to her room, but there was absolutely nothing to do, and she was wide awake. She decided to chance it.

Her heart was pounding hard as she descended step after step. She held her breath, deathly afraid that even that could be heard in the stillness of an empty house. She reached the second floor landing and quickly made her way down the rest. She fast-walked to the library and entered. She lit a couple of lamps and looked over the book titles.

It took her more than an hour to narrow her choices down to two books: Daniel Dafoe's *Moll Flanders* and John Cleland's *Fanny Hill* or *Memoirs of a Woman of Pleasure*. Both novels were about the choices of young women who found themselves in difficult circumstances and what challenges faced them.

She picked up both books, hoping to find some direction for her life. She finally decided on *Fanny Hill*, and had been reading it for about an hour when she heard the front door open and close.

She looked up from her book, unsure if she heard what she thought she heard. She listened closely. She heard something again. Cadence was either walking around, or someone was in the house. She wondered if the real killer had come back to kill her and Cadence. Her heart rate shot up again.

She crawled under the table she was sitting at, just in

case the intruder saw the light and came into the library. She heard footsteps going up the stairs and assumed it was Tristan Bouvier. She let out a sigh of relief. Her heart rate slowed to normal. First, she looked through the glass panes, but couldn't see much.

Quietly, she opened the door and looked out. She saw a figure climbing the stairs, but couldn't tell who it was. She stepped out of the library to confirm that it was Tristan; otherwise, she wouldn't be able to relax knowing someone was creeping around the house. But the figure was already gone. She went to the stairs and looked. Again he was gone.

"Joshua, is that you?" she heard Cadence say.

Lauren's eyes nearly bulged out of her head when she heard that. She gasped and covered her mouth. Her heart thudded feverishly.

"Yeah, it's me," Joshua said. "Where's Lauren?"

Chapter 49

"Let's do it again."

Lauren couldn't believe what she was hearing. This new development was so unexpected. She would have bet her life that Tristan was the killer. Now she knew differently. It was Joshua all along, just as Aubrey had suspected. Her heart was pounding again. She shook her head, thinking, *They were in on it together.* Together they had killed eight men in two days. If it were possible, her heart pounded even harder when she realized that if they didn't hesitate to kill eight men, one of them her husband, they wouldn't hesitate to kill her and come up with a crazy story that she had tried to kill Cadence.

Suddenly, she was glad that she hadn't told Joshua what her plans were; otherwise, she would be dead now too. She kept her hand over her mouth, scared to death they might hear her. If they discovered her, she would have to dig her own grave.

She wanted to run to her room just in case they decided to check on her, but she was compelled to listen to them to see what was really going on.

"She's sleeping," Cadence answered.

Gingerly, she climbed a few stairs, stood on her toes, and peeked up into the room. She could see everything. Joshua and Cadence were kissing passionately.

When they came up for air, Cadence said, "I can't believe we did it."

"Did you break it off with Tristan like I told you?" Joshua demanded.

"Yes, yes, you know I did," Cadence said. "I love you so."

After that, the talk ended and the action began. Cadence, who was already naked, tore open Joshua's shirt. While he finished removing his shirt, she yanked down his pants. He didn't have on any underwear. Now they were both completely nude, groping one another as they lost all control. With ease, he picked up the petite blonde and eased her onto his plow. A guttural groan found its way out of her mouth.

Without looking, Joshua reached back and closed the door. The light went out, and both the bed and the people in it howled like wolves for more than an hour.

While they were making love like animals in heat, Lauren thought it best that she go back to the library and put everything back the way she found it. Then she went back up the stairs and listened to them grunt and groan.

Hearing people have sex was exciting. It was incredibly funny at times, listening to two people who were totally uninhibited, saying raunchy things in the heat of passion. But that wasn't why she was there. She had heard her mom and dad have sex for years, and when they finished, they always talked. That's why she was there—to hear their pillow talk.

Lauren knew the talking would begin soon, because the grunting and groaning was slowing. The bedsprings were far less noisy, so she listened intensely.

"So, when do you find out what's in the will?" Joshua asked.

"Tomorrow," Cadence said. "I'll stop by on the way to my shop. I'm taking Lauren with me. I like her. Do you?"

"Beautiful girl," Joshua said.

Lauren was unmoved by his compliment. She already knew she was beautiful, and had known it long before she came to America. His acknowledgment of the obvious was not a revelation.

Cadence noticed that he had avoided the question, and that was a potential problem. "You better not bed her."

"It never even crossed my mind," he said.

"Stop lying. She's beautiful, so I know you've been thinking about it."

"Well, maybe a little," he joked. "But I love you, Cadence. We're in this thing together, okay? All the way, right?"

"Right, but we have to be careful," she said. "We don't want people getting suspicious. We don't want them asking questions. We want it all to go away, and we can start all over like nothing ever happened.

"I'm going to make you my new driver. That way we can see each other all the time without attracting attention. You can move in and everything; live just like Aubrey and the rest of Beaumont's men."

"I don't mind driving you around, but I can't move into the house. Besides, what about Lauren? She might see or hear something if I'm here. Plus, I don't want the field workers to think I've changed."

"What if I put Lauren in the slave quarters? Then you could move in."

"No. It would look like you got rid of her so we could be together."

"I could take her into my confidence. That way, if she knows, she can help cover for us."

"Can the girl be trusted?"

"Who's she gonna tell, Joshua? Who does she know?"

"I don't know about letting the girl in on this thing, Cadence. I don't. That's something we have to really be careful on."

"Well, we'll figure it out later. As I said, tomorrow I'm taking her with me to town, and I'll feel her out and see if she can be trusted."

"So, I'm driving you to town tomorrow?"

"Yes."

"You think he left you everything in the will?"

"Most of it. I'm sure he left Marie-Elise and Tristan something."

"What are you going to do if he didn't?"

"You mean if he left it to Tristan or Marie-Elise?"

"Yeah. I can handle Tristan, but Marie-Elise is going to be a problem. Her and Walker would love to take over Bouvier Hill."

"If Tristan or Marie-Elise get the property and some-how they die, who would get the property then?"

"I really don't know. I suppose it would fall to me then."

"How far are you willing to go?"

"You mean, am I willing to kill again?"

"Yes."

"Yes. Are you?"

"I'm in this thing all the way."

"Me too," she cooed.

"Okay, well, I better get outta here."

"Let's do it again."

When Lauren heard that, she knew it was time to go to her room. Tomorrow she would act like she knew absolutely nothing.

She got in the bed and thought about all that she'd heard, and wondered what Walker Tresvant and Marie-Elise would think if they knew what was going on. She wanted to tell them, but she couldn't trust them either. She never felt more alone than she felt at that moment. She was in a world where everyone had ulterior motives. She realized that if she were to survive, she had to be cunning, just like they were. She decided she would keep her eyes and ears open, but her mouth shut.

Chapter 50

"You're not in the will. Sorry."

Julian Bailey's law office was located on the upper end of Royal Street. The carriage stopped in front of the office at precisely nine o'clock. Joshua jumped down from his lofty perch and opened the carriage door for Mrs. Bouvier. That's who she was to him in public anyway.

Cadence was wearing a black dress and bonnet. She told Lauren to wait in the carriage for her, and then she went into the office. Joshua could see her through the picture window. She was sitting in the outer office. A few seconds later, Tristan Bouvier and his wife arrived. Not long after that, Walker Tresvant and Marie-Elise made their grand entrance.

"So, how you like livin' in the big house, Lauren?" Joshua asked.

Lauren got out of the carriage to stretch her legs. "It's okay, I suppose."

"Okay? Bouvier Manor is one of the best houses in New Orleans. And you say it's *okay?*"

"Maybe I chose the wrong words," Lauren said. "I have not been here very long, so I'm still uncomfortable. I don't know anyone. I don't have any friends. I'm all alone here. So, even though Bouvier Manor is a really nice place, I don't feel at home. You know what I mean?"

He looked her up and down and said, "Yeah, girl, I know what you mean. If you feelin' lonely, maybe you could come down to my cabin sometime and we could talk."

Lauren remembered what she'd heard him say about her the night before. She also remembered what Cadence had said too. Here he was violating what she had told him already.

"I'm spoken for, Joshua," she said.

"Spoken for? You just said you was alone and lonely," he said. "I'm extending a hand of friendship out to you, if you want it."

"Excuse me," a man wearing a gray suit said. "Are you Lauren Renee Bouvier?"

She turned around and looked at the man. "I am now, sir."

"Uh, could you come in here?" the man said. "This concerns you too."

"What concerns me, sir?" she asked.

"I'm sorry, Lauren. My name is Julian Bailey. I'm Beaumont Bouvier's attorney and the executor of his last will and testament."

"You're the what again, sir?" she said sincerely. "I'm

new here. I speak the language, but I don't understand everything I hear."

"I am the executor. Basically, it's my job to make sure that Beaumont Bouvier's last wishes are carried out to the letter."

"Okay, but I still don't understand why I need to be in there. I'm not a member of the family. As a matter of fact, I just got here a few days ago."

Julian smiled and said, "I know, but he put you in his will anyway. Remember the day he stopped here on this street, in front of this office?"

"Not really, sir."

"Well, you do remember stopping somewhere and having to wait for a while, right?"

"Yes, sir."

"Well, that's what he was doing. Come on in. I think you're going to be pleased."

"Uh, what about me, Monsieur Bailey?" Joshua asked.

"You're Joshua, right?" Bailey asked.

"Right, sir." Joshua smiled.

"You're not in the will. Sorry," Bailey said.

Chapter 51

"But why me, Monsieur Bailey?"

The atmosphere in Julian Bailey's office was thick and full of venom. The Tresvant and Bouvier families were beside themselves with anger, and the will had yet to be read. The idea of Lauren Renee being in the will at all drove them to the edge of insanity. They would have understood to some degree if Aubrey or any of the other housemen were in the will. In fact, they expected as much. But Lauren had only been on the shores of the country for three days. They didn't understand how she could get anything, even if it were a penny. As far as they were concerned, it was a slap in their faces that she was there to hear the will read.

Julian escorted Lauren to her seat, which was right next to Cadence. Lauren thought she heard her growl when she sat down. She looked at Cadence and thought, *I'm next. She's going to kill me for this.*

"I guess we can get started now that we're all here," Julian said. "It's a rather simple will. Clear. Concise. To the point." He cleared his throat, knowing full well that what they were about to hear was going to take their anger to another level.

"Beaumont wrote a letter that I'm supposed to read before explaining how all his assets are divided."

Tristan said, "Who cares what he had to say? I don't like having to sit here with one of our servants, and I certainly don't want to sit here any longer than I have to. So please, skip his vitriolic drivel and tell us how he split up the estate."

"If I don't read his letter to you all, if any one of you leaves before I finish it, all of you forfeit anything you had coming."

"Who gets the money and property in that case?" Walker asked.

"Lauren gets it all—everything."

Tristan and Cadence nearly leapt out of their skin. They both stood up at the same time and in unison screamed, "What!"

Tristan, looking at Lauren, yelled, "This is an outrage!"

"Tristan, please," Christine said. "Let's hear what your brother had to say. It'll be okay, I'm sure."

He sat down and composed himself.

Expecting that reaction, Julian maintained his cool and calmly said, "I think you heard me, or better still, I think you heard Beaumont loud and clear. Now . . . do I read this . . . or do you leave this office with the clothes on your backs?"

Completely deflated, Cadence melted in her seat and

almost in a trance, babbled, "You mean we wouldn't even be allowed to pack anything from Bouvier Manor? My clothes, my jewelry, nothing?"

Julian leaned back in his chair and said, "That's correct. Well, you'd get to keep your clothing shop, but you'd receive no support from the estate."

"What about me?" Tristan said. "Would I at least keep my home and possessions?"

"No. Your children would be provided for, but that's it."

"Damn him!" Tristan said. "I hope the Molly burns in hell forever and ever!"

"And me? What if I leave?" Marie-Elise said without passion.

"You get nothing. Walker is your husband, and it's his responsibility to provide for you."

"Monsieur Bailey," Lauren said, "surely I can leave. This is a family affair. I should not be here."

"You can leave, Lauren, but if you do, they lose it and I get it. Like it or not, you have to be here so they can get their share. He was very specific about that."

"But why me, Monsieur Bailey? I just don't understand."

"You'll understand when I finish the letter and the will. Now, what's it going to be?" He eyed them all for a few silent seconds. "Do I get to keep an estate worth eight hundred thousand dollars a year? Or do you all want your share of it? It's up to you."

Silence.

"By your silence, I take it you want me to read the letter. Here goes."

Chapter 52

Dear Family,

Hmmm. Family? I have often wondered if the term even applies to us as a unit. Perhaps it does, as we do have the same blood—except, I suppose, for Aubrey and my other house servants. But I do think of Aubrey and the others as family; more family than my wife, and certainly my younger brother, Tristan.

As for my sister, Marie-Elise, I love you more than you will ever know. I was never disgraced by your choice of husband. That was father, never me. I was always proud of your courage to do as you pleased, not as society expected or even demanded. But, alas, you are fortunate that you made your choice in New Orleans, where free people of color are plenteous and the intermingling of the races are commonplace. Had you done the same elsewhere, you may have been hanged. Never lose sight of that, my dear.

In any case, I leave you the bulk of the Bouvier estate,

which includes Bouvier Manor, Bouvier Hill, and Bouvier Sugar. In addition to this, I leave you sixty percent of everything, including all of the above, and the liquid assets.

I do this knowing full well that Walker is sitting there now as this letter is being read, thinking of how he can get the rest of Bouvier Sugar and the property. Perhaps a merger is the smart move now that I am no longer alive. Do what you will, and always remember I loved you until death knocked. Death, however, will not diminish my favor or my love for you. I was never ever embarrassed by any decision you made. I wish you and my dear brother-in-law, Walker Tresvant, all the best.

Now to my younger brother, Tristan. You have always been an embarrassment to the Bouvier name. You've added nothing to our legacy, and have only taken. I suspect your progeny will be equally slothful and needy, thinking the world owes them something. But, you are my brother no matter what you've done to me, to my wife, to your wife, and to yourself.

I suppose you and Cadence, the whore who pretended to be a wife, thought you were fooling everybody. You should know that you fool no one, except perhaps Christine, who adores you and worships the very ground you walk on. For the life of me, I never understood why. At this point, I don't need to.

For your treachery, you will receive nothing—no percentage of Bouvier Hill, Bouvier Manor, Bouvier Sugar, and no percentage of the liquid assets. You will have no association whatsoever with the family business. You will, however, be taken care of for the remainder of your days on earth.

As I said, you are my brother. But, if the day ever comes

and it is discovered that you are not my blood brother, and I sincerely hope it does, you will be cut off completely; you and your children with Christine. The children you sired with the whore who pretended to be my wife, Cadence, well, that's another story. They will be cared for despite her longtime adulterous affair with you.

And now for the whore who pretended to by my wife, Cadence. You are still quite beautiful, and so I guess you shall not be alone forever. I can only hope that my letting the proverbial cat out of the bag in Christine's presence has irreparably destroyed your diabolical alliance with Tristan.

As my brother is my brother no matter what, you are my wife no matter what, and so I will not completely destroy you. My dear Cadence, you have always sought power and control, and you shall finally have it. But it comes at a price.

First, you can never marry, unless you marry a Bouvier by blood. This excludes Tristan, as you may actually love him, which would put poor Christine in danger. If you love Tristan, I have no doubt that you would figure out a way to rid yourself of her to pursue your own base ends.

Perhaps you'll marry a younger Bouvier, who will fulfill your every longing. You're still beautiful and you have the bosoms to attract just about any man. Or perhaps your lust for power will keep you alone. Perhaps you'll live in sin so that you maintain power. Whatever you do, try to be happy doing it.

Second, while Bouvier Hill is yours to control, you must answer to my beloved sister, which means you will have to answer to Walker Tresvant. I know that hurt, didn't it, dear? But wait; there's more to come.

I am leaving you thirty percent of everything; however, to get it, you must relinquish your beloved clothing store, which I purchased for you so you would stop trying to run my business. Bouvier Hill is a fulltime position. Do not treat it like a bordello.

If you decide to keep the store, you forfeit Bouvier Hill and the power you so desperately crave. You must decide now, by the conclusion of the reading of the will. Also, if you do choose the clothing store, you must leave Bouvier Manor immediately and permanently. You will finally be completely on your own and call all the shots. Your thirty percent will be given to my sweet sister, Marie-Elise.

A final note to my family, and especially you, Walker: if and when a merger takes place between Bouvier Sugar and Tresvant Sugar, both names must now and forever be a part of the brand name. To be clear, the names are never ever to be changed, as they are our legacy, the proof to our posterity that we lived, succeeded, and thrived—both houses. And because we lived, they now enjoy the fruits of our collective labor.

I'm sure you're dying to know why I want both names to remain in perpetuity. It is because Damien Bouvier created in Alexander Tresvant Bouvier, his former slave, the drive necessary to become what he became. I will not regurgitate the messy details of how it happened, but it did. Dropping the Bouvier name cannot repudiate this fact.

I apologize for his ruthless behavior two generations ago. Now, we will all go down in history as one family. The Tresvants will be a large branch of the tree of life that Damien spawned through lust. Personally, I think it fitting that it turned out this way—it's almost righteous.

Last, but not least, to my dear house servants, I leave the remaining ten percent. Each servant is to receive one percent, and the rest goes to my closest friend, Aubrey Bouvier. If any of the house servants die, his share goes to Aubrey. If Aubrey dies, the percentage is to be divided among the survivors. If there are no survivors, the remaining ten percent goes to Marie-Elise.

Effective upon the reading of this letter, all my house servants are free. They, too, must keep the Bouvier name or they forfeit their shares. They must also remain in New Orleans. I have not freed them so that some greedy slaver can claim them again.

The surviving house servants will be given Bouvier Manor, or they will be given the clothing store, whichever Cadence decides to give up. Their formal educations, homes, and businesses will be paid for by the Bouvier estate. Once their businesses, or whatever endeavors they so choose are established, they will be on their own. No further help will be given to them without the say so of Marie-Elise.

The ten percent due the house servants is payable immediately. To be clear, the house servants are to immediately have eighty thousand dollars divided according to the manner I already outlined. The house servants shall receive ten percent of Bouvier Sugar or Bouvier Tresvant Sugar in perpetuity.

I love you all. May the Bouvier and Tresvant names live on forevermore.

Beaumont Bouvier

Chapter 53

"What about your money?"

When Julian Bailey finished reading Beaumont's letter, he looked at them to get their reaction. First he looked at Tristan and Christine. They were both hurt and confused. They obviously expected more. As he watched Christine, her expression seemed to morph into shock. She was no doubt surprised by the revelation of adultery and children with her sister-in-law.

Cadence, on the other hand, was dissatisfied, but not overwhelmed by it. She probably thought thirty percent and finally being the boss was better than nothing.

Walker Tresvant and Marie-Elise were beside themselves with joy, while the young woman that didn't feel she belonged with the family was subdued.

"What's wrong, Lauren?" Julian said.

"I don't think I understand, sir," she said.

"What don't you understand?" Julian asked.

"Well, I think the letter said something about me being free," she said. "Is that right?"

Tristan flung a profanity-laced tirade at Lauren and stormed out. He was outraged at the sum of money and benefits she had received. Christine followed him, but she wasn't upset at all. She was probably still in shock and unsure if there was any truth to what was read to them. She was too much of a lady to make a scene. She maintained her dignity by keeping silent. When she walked out, she walked out proudly, as class and grace oozed from her pores.

"Yes, Lauren, you certainly are free," Julian said. "Do you understand the restrictions?"

"Restrictions? What do you mean?"

"Beaumont wanted you to keep your freedom, so he wants you to stay here, in New Orleans. I know you only recently arrived on the Windward, but if you leave New Orleans permanently, you could be captured again. Beaumont didn't want that for you, or any of his house servants. He also gave you a thriving business and a substantial amount of money. There are numerous free people of color here. Stick around awhile and see for yourself."

"So I'm free to go right now if I want?"

"Yes," Walker said. "But don't. I agree with Julian and Beaumont. I advise you to stay for a few months and see how you like it. I understand that you haven't seen your family for a while and they are worried sick, I'm sure. But if you go in search of them, there's no guarantee you won't be captured again.

"Even if you get back to Africa, there's no guarantee your family will be there. For all you know, they are on their way here. If they are, you can buy their freedom and you can all stay. Think about it."

"How do I get to the Isle of Santo Domingo?" she asked.

"What's on the Isle of Santo Domingo?" Walker asked.

"Amir. We were to be married before our capture. We both made promises. I intend to keep mine."

"Listen, Lauren. I don't think you understand the situation because you're from another land," Marie-Elise said. "Ten percent of a thriving company has just fallen into your lap. Do you have any idea what you can do with eighty thousand dollars cash in New Orleans? And the idea that you'll get at least that or more until you die doesn't appeal to you? And then your children will get it.

"The dress shop alone could be worth a fortune if you work hard and turn it into something. I mean, you've already got clients lined up. What with the octoroon ball just a month or two away, women will be storming the place, needing gowns and all the things women need."

"Lauren," Cadence interrupted, "I'm going back to Bouvier Hill. Are you coming with me, or are you staying with your new friends?"

"I take it you've decided to take Beaumont's offer of running Bouvier Hill and Sugar?" Julian asked.

"Yes, I've accepted."

"So then," Julian continued, "you'll be turning the keys over to Lauren immediately?"

Cadence's face twisted into a menacing scowl. "I suppose you want me to show her around too?"

"That would be the ladylike thing to do, Cadence."

"Well, I'm leaving right now. If you want to see the place, you better come along. There's nothing in that letter that says anything about me having to show you anything. What I do now, I do out of respect for Beaumont."

When Lauren heard what Cadence said about respecting Beaumont, she wanted to strangle her. She had no love for Beaumont, but he did set her free, and that gesture made her feel badly about the way his life ended. She thought Beaumont's life should be avenged, since the real killers had not paid for their crimes. She would see to it, but it would take time.

"Okay, let's go," Lauren said. "Show me the clothing store."

"Lauren," Walker said, "what about your money?"

"Oh yeah." She looked at Julian. "Can I get it later?"

"Sure," Julian said. "When you return, I'll take you to the bank and help you open an account, okay?"

Chapter 54

"And this is for you. "

Six months passed and Lauren was still in New Orleans, still living on Bouvier Hill as a free woman of color. She decided to stay because there was much truth to what Walker Tresvant said. There was no guarantee that she would ever get back to Nigeria; and if she did make it back, she wasn't sure her family would still be there.

The one thing she knew for sure was that she wasn't the same person who was taken, and she never would be again. But still, she felt a longing for home, a burning desire to see her mother and father, her sisters and brothers, and all the people of Dahomey. A day didn't go by that she didn't think of her family and Amir. She imagined that they were fine, living their lives, enjoying themselves, but never forgetting Ibo Atikah Mustafa, the seventh daughter of the first wife.

She was becoming more and more American with each passing day, having learned arithmetic, the clothing business, and the value of a dollar. On occasion, she would get angry with herself for enjoying life in America so much. It didn't make sense to her. Why would God allow her to be kidnapped and brought to the shores of North America—New Orleans, specifically—only to set her free three days later?

She had given much thought to the number three. It took three months to get to the Isle of Santo Domingo; three months to get to the shores of North America. Her father had three wives. Her relationship with Amir was threefold: Ibo, Amir, and Adesola. Captain Rutgers' marriage was threefold: Joseph, Tracy, and Jonah. Beaumont's marriage was threefold: Beaumont, Cadence, and Tristan. The resurrection happened after three days. They all needed to forgive and be forgiven, she realized.

Those realizations made her reexamine the night she took flight and the consequences of that decision. When she thought about all that befell her, her love for Amir, the voyage, Captain Rutgers, the murders aboard the Windward and at Bouvier Hill, she would never let the words spill out of her mouth, but she was glad it had all happened the way it had. She knew there was a higher purpose in it, but she didn't know what it would be. She had often wondered if God truly existed and now, in her own heart, she knew he did. Nevertheless, she still didn't understand him or his methods.

She now had plenty of money, but it came from slave labor. Hundreds of people were on the Windward. Many died on the way to America; she didn't. Why? Women were brutally raped; she wasn't. Why? She was purchased and set free by a homosexual. Why? It would have made more sense to her if she had been purchased by a member of the clergy and set free. Why didn't it happen that way?

Beaumont Bouvier had done right by her in the end, and yet he had been slaughtered. Why? So far, nothing had happened to Cadence and Joshua for the murders they committed. Why? Would Beaumont, Aubrey, and the others ever get justice? If so, who would be their avenging angel? These and many other questions clung to her, forcing her to think of why she was in New Orleans.

She had promised Amir that she would come for him if she ever had the means. She didn't dare leave New Orleans, but with help from Marie-Elise, she hired an attorney to go to the Isle of Santo Domingo and buy Amir if he could be found alive.

She had done that three months ago. She had been expecting a ship for nearly a week, and it had finally arrived. She was on her way to the docks to see if the attorney was on this ship. She had been disappointed several times. She hoped it would be different this time.

Seeing the Windward docked and being unloaded was bittersweet. She'd had firsthand experience on the ship, so she knew what the slaves had endured. But still, she was glad to see a familiar face coming down the gangplank.

She tried not to smile when she saw Captain Rutgers disembarking. After all, he was the man who had brought her to New Orleans and told Beaumont to buy her. She couldn't help herself, though. Six months of living well had dulled her senses to the idea of slavery, because she was greatly benefiting from it. For those reasons, the peculiar institution was almost acceptable.

She remembered her first day in New Orleans, the day

she witnessed Kimba's savage lashing and subsequent sub-
jugation. Now she thought Kimba shouldn't have tried to
run away. Six months of living off the backs of slaves had
altered her sense of right and wrong; yet she had no problem determining the guilt of Cadence and Joshua. As far
as she was concerned, they had to answer for that.

She waved at Rutgers, and he did likewise as he made
his way over to greet her. As expected, Jonah, his brother,
approached him. Jonah was trying to talk to him, but Rutgers kept walking, and never even looked at him. It was as if
he couldn't hear him, like he didn't exist. It was a cruel
thing to do and a difficult thing to watch, yet she understood how Rutgers felt and agreed. His brother had crossed
a bridge that he didn't know was burning behind him.

"Well, hello," Rutgers said like they were old dear
friends who hadn't seen each other in more than a
decade. "You'll never guess who's onboard."

"Amir!" she said with unbridled excitement.

"He'll be coming at any moment," Rutgers said.

"Is he well?"

"He is well."

"Ibo!" Amir exclaimed when he saw her.

She looked up and saw him running down the gangplank. Seeing his smile warmed her heart. Without excus-
ing herself, she ran to him and he to her. They embraced
and held on tight. The love they had for each other had
survived.

"I'm told that you are wealthy now," Amir said in
Yoruba, their native tongue. "Is it true?"

"It is," she said, speaking the same language, unable to
hide the joy that bubbled beneath the surface.

"Come," she said. "I have so much to tell you."

"As do I," he said. "I want to hear it all."

"Do you still want to marry me?" she asked. "I am still a maiden—your maiden, if you still want me."

"I do want you, Ibo. Virgin or not." He kissed her. "I love you so."

"I love you too," she said and kissed him back.

"I've learned so much. I now understand my mother and why she was willing to sacrifice her life for us. She found peace, and so have I. In exchange for peace, I have forgiven Captain Rutgers. I am forever free now. Have you found peace, my love? Please tell me you have."

Before she could answer, a man she had often seen at the docks whenever she was there walked up to them. He smiled and said, "Excuse me, good sir. Did you just arrive from the Isle of Santo Domingo?"

Lauren was about to answer when Amir said, "I've learned to speak English." He looked at the man, smiled, and said, "I was on the island, sir, yes. It's beautiful there. Have you ever been?"

"That's what I thought," the man said. "And this is for you."

He pulled out a pistol and *bang!* He blew Amir's brains clean out of his head and all over Lauren.

Everything had happened in slow motion. She had seen it, but she could not believe it. Amir stood perfectly still for a few seconds as his eyes lost their light. Then, as if in slow motion, the rest of him realized he was dead and floated to the ground, making no effort to brace the fall.

"Noooo!" Lauren screamed.

The man leaned over Amir's dead body and screamed,

"That was for Francois and Helen Torvell! Helen was my sister, and you savages raped and killed her!"

Pow! Another shot rang out.

Captain Rutgers had killed the man, blowing his brains clean out of his head. "And that was for killing an innocent man." Then he fell to his knees and wept bitterly. "This was my last contract. I was finished after this."

Jonah, who had seen it all, walked over to his brother and stood next to him. He never said a word. He just looked down at his brother.

Joseph could sense someone was staring at him. He turned to see who it was. When he saw his brother's compassion, Joseph wrapped his arms around his legs and said, "I forgive you, Jonah."

Just like that, the bitterness he had held on to for decades, fled.

Just like that, bitterness entered the heart of Lauren Renee Bouvier, and it would be with her for a long time.

Author's Note

Thinking back on it, my most vivid memories of a love for stories came from two sources: high school literature and movies. I took literature when I was fifteen because it was supposed to be an easy A. After all, the only requirement was reading a few books, right? Uh, no. Not only did the teacher expect her students to read the books she assigned, she expected her students to figure out what the authors meant by what they wrote.

I was a sophomore attending Jesup W. Scott High School, home of the Bulldogs (All for Scott, stand up and holla.) Scott was a predominately black school, but my literature teacher was a white female. I wish I knew who she was and where she is today; she would be the first teacher of all my academic teachers I'd hug and thank for her attention to detail and her ability to take a story apart, piece by piece, and explain it to the neophyte. She was the person who taught me to look beyond the obvious and see the message behind the words.

What I enjoy reading most is biographies of famous people and nonfiction Mafia books. I'm currently reading Diahann Carroll's *The Legs Are the Last to Go: Aging, Acting, Marrying & Other Things I Learned the Hard Way*. I'm really enjoying it. Not only is she the most beautiful woman that ever lived (that's right, I said it), she is one of the most overlooked bright and burning lights the African American community ever produced. She is the epitome of class and elegance, and I wish more African American women knew and emulated the best in her.

Anyway, back to my little soliloquy.

I'm often asked in emails and on book tours how I came up with the character Johnnie Wise. I must admit that I think a lot of women come to my signings because they do not believe a man actually wrote the series—that's what many say in emails and in person. The truth of how I created Johnnie Wise is not a sexy story, but here goes:

I needed a villain to say some very nasty things to a character named Terry Morretti, a major character in my first novel, *Fate's Redemption*. If you all know anything about any of my novels, you know that I bring in all the races, sexes, politics, religion, sports, martial arts, music, and everything else I see and read about. *Fate's Redemption* is no exception. Terry Morretti was a white woman with Italian and Cherokee bloodlines. She fell in love with a black man of considerable wealth and education—William Wise, Johnnie's nephew and Benny's son. The black women in his family—some of them anyway—hated her and women like her for daring to do so.

As you know, I try very hard to tell the truth in fiction. I know that's an oxymoron, but it is what I believe in. It is what I believe my high school literature teacher was trying to teach me—to look behind the words, for there, the real story lies.

I'm sure that some of the people who read *Fate's Redemption* didn't like the truth I told, but I told it anyway, much like I do with all my novels. The trick is to see if you can discover what truth I'm telling. There are always two truths in my stories: the obvious truth and the hidden truth. The obvious truth is for you, the fans. The hidden truth is my need to speak.

In the aforementioned novel, Ms. Morretti is to meet the black family on Thanksgiving, and she's ambushed by some of the women in the main character's family. They corner the poor woman and give her a severe tongue-lashing. The women are led by none other than the famous Johnnie Wise. In *Fate's Redemption* she only appears for a few minutes. She serves my purpose, and off I go with the telling of the story.

Well . . . wouldn't you know that many of the women in Toledo, Ohio, my hometown, didn't like the outspoken Johnnie Wise?

I thought that was so unfair—so unfair, in fact, that I decided to go back in time and write a novel showing how a person could become so cruel. But a strange thing happened. As I was writing the story, I got ideas for about ten to twenty books—or more, if the fans demanded them. *The Diary of Josephine Baptiste* is just one of them.

Every character in every novel should have a beginning, a middle, and an end. Just like a real person's life, we are born, become middle-aged, and then we die. I understand this, and so I believe that any character I create, no matter how small, has a beginning, a middle, and an ending.

Anyway, I've got less than an hour to finish this and send it to the publisher, so I better move on. Perhaps I'll tell you all more about the novels in a future author's note.

The other major influence in my life of stories is movies. I love them more than books. Believe it or not, I'd rather see a good movie that I've seen dozens of times than watch a pro football game. And I'm a huge NFL fan. I used to live across the street from a movie theater that was in the heart of the ghetto. I lived in an apartment over an establishment that served liquor. It was called the Doorbell Bar, if I'm not mistaken. I suppose I should ask my mother, but she's not here (smiling) and I have what, about fifty minutes left to finish this.

Anyway, I went to the movies every Saturday without fail. I would stay in there all day long. I'd watch the same movies over and over again. Most of the time, it would be a double feature of some sort. And of course, they would show reels of the Three Stooges, or vampire and werewolf shorts. Sometimes they'd show Bugs Bunny cartoons. I had a marvelous time.

What I didn't know was that all those films were honing the God-given gift of storytelling already in me. I truly believe that's why people tell me my books are cinematic and read like films.

What you should all know is that I was almost destroyed by my composition teacher when I transferred to a predominately white school, Robert S. Rogers. I was taking an English course, and I had written a paper that I was quite proud of.

To understand this story, you must first understand that I was a very poor student. I rarely cracked open a book that wasn't a novel. I graduated at nearly the bottom of my class. I think there were like 530 graduates; I think I was 529. Frankly, I think the faculty got together and said, "Let's get rid of this guy!" Just kidding, but I did graduate with a D+ average, I think.

Anyway, the teacher, a white male, unlike my white female teacher at the predominately black school, used my paper as a vivid example of how not to write. I had gotten a big fat F on my paper. I was the only black person in the class. The year was 1976. This guy did a real number on me, and the white kids were literally falling out of their chairs laughing at me. I was so hurt by this that I got up, walked out of his class, never to return.

To his credit, he found me walking the halls later that week and apologized, but it was too late. I was so embarrassed that I couldn't go back to the class and look into the faces of my white classmates.

From that moment forward, I had no plans to be a good student or even to read again. It wasn't until twenty some odd years later that I went back. This time, I was a grown man; strong of mind, strong of spirit. And wouldn't you know it, the same thing nearly happened again. Two more white English teachers—two males, this time—predominately white college, literature teacher vs. fiction writing teacher.

I am running out of time, so I will have to cut this story

short. Suffice it to say, the literature teacher, whether he knew it or not, was a source of discouragement. The fiction writing teacher was a huge source of encouragement. I was not going to school to become a novelist. I happened to fall into it because of the above scenario. One man nearly ruined me for life and probably has no idea what damage he'd done.

Twenty some odd years later, another white man mended and healed wounds sustained two decades earlier. There's so much more I could say, but due to time constraints, I'll sum up everything by saying *The Little Black Girl Lost* series arose from an unusual set of circumstances over the course of nearly thirty years.

My point is this: Don't give up on your hopes and dreams. Know what you want out of life, and diligently pursue it in spite of all that would come against you. I am living proof that no force of nature can break your will to succeed. The will . . . is surrendered.

Until next time, keep buying the books that you love.

Wishing you all the best in all things good,
Keith Lee Johnson